"Just what do you think you were doing?"

Becca shrank back, but couldn't get away. "I wasn't doing anything. He—"

"I know what he was doing," Nick said, cutting her off. "And I know what you were doing. Do you enjoy leading guys on? Like you did to me ten years ago?"

Too late to take the blurted, angry words back, Nick wondered what he could say that would stop the tears that filled her eyes. He hated himself.

Everything happened too fast. Instantly she was across the room, grabbing her coat from the hook on the wall. "My family will get by somehow. I don't need this job."

"Becca, wait. I didn't mean it. Please. Let me—"

But she was out the door, slamming it behind her.

Dear Reader,

According to the U.S. Census Bureau's 2004 report, there are 10 million single mothers living with children under eighteen in the United States. There are several reasons for a woman being a single mother, and Becca Tyler's story covers one of them.

Being a single mom myself for the past few years, I've seen and learned just how hard it can be. But there are also many joys to experience, whether a mother is single or part of a nuclear family. And although my girls were much older than Becca's three children when I started down the path of single motherhood, the struggles and rewards are much the same. Those rewards are what make it worthwhile.

For Becca, a strength she didn't know she had as well as her love for her children kept her going. When Nick Morelli returned, he helped by providing a means for her to take a step up and take control of her life. Sometimes that's all we need.

It's the little things in life that count the most—a smile from a child, sunshine after a storm, a friend who lends a hand. Whether you're a single mom, a mom with a loving partner, or someone hoping to be a mom someday, I hope you'll enjoy *Family by Design* as much as I enjoyed getting to know Becca and Nick.

It's such a pleasure to be a part of the Harlequin American Romance community!

Best wishes and happy reading!

Roxann Delaney

Family by Design
ROXANN DELANEY

Special
Treat!

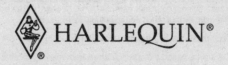

TORONTO • NEW YORK • LONDON
AMSTERDAM • PARIS • SYDNEY • HAMBURG
STOCKHOLM • ATHENS • TOKYO • MILAN • MADRID
PRAGUE • WARSAW • BUDAPEST • AUCKLAND

ISBN-13: 978-0-373-75198-3
ISBN-10:   0-373-75198-2

FAMILY BY DESIGN

www.eHarlequin.com

Printed in U.S.A.

ABOUT THE AUTHOR

Roxann Delaney doesn't remember a time when she wasn't reading or writing, and she always loved that touch of romance in both. A native Kansan, she's lived on a farm, in a small town and has returned to live in the city where she was born. Her four daughters and grandchildren keep her busy when she isn't writing, designing Web sites, or planning her high school class reunions. The 1999 Maggie Award winner is excited about being a part of Harlequin American Romance and loves to hear from readers. Contact her at roxann@roxanndelaney.com or visit her Web site www.roxanndelaney.com.

In memory of Charlie DeNosky, who will be greatly missed by his family and his many friends.

Chapter One

Becca Tyler limped her car to the side of the road, the vehicle lurching every few inches because of the flat tire. Coming to a final, slow stop, she turned off the engine and pressed her forehead against the smooth, cold leather on the steering wheel.

What now?

She'd left her two kids and baby, Daisy, with her best friend, then driven the thirty miles from Katyville to an all-night pharmacy in Wichita to buy a vaporizer for the baby. Daisy's cold had gotten worse, and her raspy breathing had Becca worried. If things didn't improve and the vaporizer didn't do the trick, she would have to take the baby to the emergency room.

One more expense she couldn't afford.

With a heavy sigh of resignation, Becca lifted her head. If she was lucky, the spare would have enough air to get her home—or at least to Raylene's house in Katyville. She'd worry about getting the flat fixed later, as soon as Daisy was breathing easier.

The car door groaned in protest when she pushed it open. Cold winter air raised goose bumps on her arms, and she wished she hadn't left home without a coat—but she was too worried with a sick baby. Gravel crunched beneath her sneakers when she stepped out onto the road. When she shoved the door closed, it groaned once more, and she winced. If she could remember, she'd ask Raylene's husband to look at it. Thank heaven Jeff didn't mind doing simple upkeep and repair on her car for nothing.

Other than the whisper of her own movements, the deserted country road was silent. There were no houses in sight, no glow of yard lights, no traffic or city blocks, just wide open Kansas farmland, darkness and silence. But even in the dark, the tire's misshapen form was visible, a testament to her bad luck. When would it end?

A coyote howled in the faraway distance, and she wrapped her arms around herself to ward off the chill of the lonely sound and the winter night. Looking up at the sky dotted with twinkling starlight, she tried to fight the feeling of aloneness that consumed her. "I can't keep this up," she whispered to the universe spread out above her. "Somehow, some way, I need some help. Please."

Out of the corner of her eye, she caught a bright flash of light. Thinking it might be the headlights of a car, she turned toward it. But instead of an approaching vehicle, what she saw caused her to gasp. A bright, broad streak of blue-white light blazed amidst the heavens from left to right. At the head, reds, blues and colors she couldn't name invaded the blackness, leaving the blue-white tail streaming behind them.

A comet? It had to be. But she'd never seen such an enormous comet in all of her stargazing. She'd never seen anything so magnificently beautiful. It both calmed and energized her.

It's only a flat tire, a voice seemed to whisper to her. Yes, she would find a way to get it taken care of, and all the rest, too. It was time to find some answers and make things better. Time to take control of her life.

As she watched, she could imagine telling Danny, her oldest child, about it. He loved to watch the news, and she'd sit with him, answering his questions—questions too old for his five years.

When the sound of a car door slamming broke the silence, she let out a shriek and spun around. She had been so mesmerized by the comet, she hadn't noticed a vehicle approaching from behind. Another chill shook her as the image of a tall, broad-shouldered man moved toward her. She willed herself to remain calm but guarded, ready to protect herself if need be.

"What the hell are you doing, lady, parking in the road?" his deep voice boomed at her.

Shaking the fear inching up her spine, she answered. "I had a flat and—" She realized that the man was vaguely familiar, and she waited as he walked toward her in the darkness. The light from the comet was fading, but as the man came closer and stopped, she stared at him, not sure if her memory was playing tricks on her. After all, it had been ten years.

"Nick? Nick Morelli?"

The scowl disappeared from his face and was replaced by a look of puzzlement. "Yeah, that's me. But who the he—" He leaned closer, taking her all in with one long look.

Becca wanted to die. All thoughts of taking control vanished. She remembered that look, remembered the heat that had flowed through her every time he had looked at her, just as it was flowing once again.

"Becca?"

Memories nearly overwhelmed her, but she managed to nod before she turned around so he couldn't see how he affected her. She had pretty much forgotten Nick, the face of her youth. Thinking about it too often reminded her of the bad choices she'd made and was determined not to make again. Her life was going to change. It had to. Not for her sake, but for her kids'.

Eyes searching, she finally found the fading tail of the comet and watched as it stretched across the black velvet sky. "Did you see the comet?" she asked over her shoulder.

But he wasn't looking at the sky. He was looking at her. Another shudder shook her.

"You're cold," he said, slipping out of his black leather jacket to drape it around her shoulders. "Don't you have enough sense not to stand out here without a coat? It's December, not July."

"It's not that cold." And it wasn't, not since he'd put his jacket around her. The warmth—*his* warmth—seeped into her.

He continued to look at her, and then spun around to make his way to her car. "You said you have a flat. Do you have a spare?"

Joining him, she pulled the coat closer, wishing she didn't need it. It smelled like Nick. The Nick she remembered. Nick, with his dark hair, dark eyes and a face that could have been chiseled by a master.

She chased the thought from her mind to answer him. "In the trunk. The jack, too. But I don't know if the spare has air."

"No way of knowing until we check it out," he said, opening the noisy car door and reaching for her keys in the ignition. The dome light shed a golden glow over his face when he turned to look at her. He wasn't happy. "Do you have a flashlight in here?"

She shook her head.

He grunted. "I'll get mine out of the truck."

While he was busy retrieving the flashlight, she wondered what he was doing so near to Katyville and decided he was probably back to visit his family over the holidays. She knew he had moved to Denver years ago. She also knew he was married. After she'd learned that, she hadn't heard anything else.

"Let's take a look at that spare."

His voice jolted her back to her senses, and she followed him to the rear of her car. But she kept her distance. Opening the trunk, he gestured for her to come closer and handed her the light. "Shine it in here."

Scrambling to stand beside him, she shone the light where he pointed. She had forgotten that the trunk light no longer worked. Inside, the baby stroller took up a large portion of the trunk, along with a few boxes. "I'll just move these," she murmured and tugged at a box with one hand.

"I'll get it," he said, and she stepped aside to give him space.

With the stroller and boxes out of the way, he found the tire, lifted it out and examined it. "It's almost as flat as the other. No reason to take the time to change them. I'll take care of them tomorrow."

"No!" She bit her lower lip, shocked at her vehemence. But she didn't want to be beholden to Nick Morelli. If it had been anyone else, she wouldn't have protested. *But it was Nick.* "I'll take care of it."

He took the light from her and helped return the boxes, and then he shined the beam in her direction. "I'll have Tony come out here and get it, first thing in the morning."

"But your brother—"

"On the house." Pocketing her keys, he slammed down the trunk lid. "If you have anything in the car you need, get it and lock the doors. I'll give you a ride home."

Since her only other choices were to stay out here on a deserted road all night or walk however many miles it was into Katyville, she didn't argue. Enough time had been wasted. Raylene would be wondering why she hadn't picked up the kids yet.

"If you can drop me at Raylene and Jeff's…" For a moment, after she had said it, she thought she had seen him raise one eyebrow, but she decided it had been nothing more than her imagination. "You remember Raylene, don't you?"

"Just give me directions when we get into town," he answered as he turned to walk away.

Opening the door to her car, she grabbed her purse and the new vaporizer, and locked up. Nick waited in his truck with the engine running, and she wondered if he still looked the same when he smiled. He hadn't smiled yet. But who could blame him? Finding a grown and weary version of a girl who had once wounded his ego wouldn't exactly make him grin.

GLAD THE LIGHTS of the small town of Katyville were in view and they were nearly there, Nick glanced at Becca beside him. He was more than surprised to see her again. And if he didn't know better, he would have thought she was scared to death of him. She sure hadn't changed much.

She had always seemed so down-to-earth, and at one time, he had thought she was something special—so special that they had planned a future together. But he had learned the truth about her a long time ago. The hard way.

"Somebody sick?" he asked, nodding toward the box she held on her lap in a death grip.

"Um, yes," she said in the quiet voice he remembered all too well. "Daisy. My baby."

Of course, she had a baby. More than one, from what he'd heard. His mother had mentioned that Becca had married some hotshot businessman her father had picked out for her. Leave it to Jock Malone to marry his daughter off to inflate his ego and raise his importance in the community even more.

He glanced at her again. "What's wrong with her? With, uh, Daisy?"

Becca shifted in the seat, hugging the box closer. "A cold."

He didn't miss the "I hope" she added under her breath, and he wondered what was going on. Nick hadn't missed the poor condition of the spare or the other tires on her car. No man should let his wife drive around in a car with bad tires. Maybe he should say something to the guy if he ever had the misfortune to meet him.

Then again, maybe he should just mind his own business. He didn't owe Becca Malone or Becca Whatever-Her-Name-Was-Now anything. He'd been in love with her once and had thought she had loved him, too. But that had been years ago, and she had managed to completely douse his ardor one late spring evening. He should've known better. At nineteen, his hormones had led his life. No more. Not only had *she* taught him a valuable lesson, but he'd also gone on to learn many more. Most of them had left their mark.

"Which way?" he asked, pulling onto the main street that ran the length of the town.

"Left at Drury, then all the way to the end of the last block."

He turned to look at her. Streetlights illuminated a face that was still young, in spite of the worry lines between her eyes and the hint of dark circles beneath them.

Not liking what he saw, he forced his attention back to the street ahead. Becca was still more than easy on the eyes, and he knew better than to get hooked on the sight of her. But the worn knees of her blue jeans and the loose edge of the shirt she wore hadn't escaped his notice. So, okay, maybe she was cleaning the bathroom or something when she hightailed it to wherever she was coming from. Or maybe she had gotten tired of dressing up for the folks in Katyville. Or maybe—

"What's your husband do for a living?" he asked suddenly, turning the corner to head down the familiar street.

"He… He's a stockbroker. Why?"

A quick glance told him that her suspicions were aroused. His damn sure were. A stockbroker made good money, and nothing about her shouted that she was living all that well, considering the well-used car she drove. If she lived in Katyville—and he guessed she did, or she wouldn't be headed in that direction so late at night—her husband probably commuted to his job in Wichita. Most people did.

"Just making conversation," he answered with a shrug.

He remained silent for the next two blocks. He hadn't done much poking around since returning to Katyville two weeks ago. Most of what he'd seen of the town was the main street, where his youngest brother owned the service station and garage that their father had owned for almost forty years.

That and the drive from his parents' home a few blocks away to the construction site at the edge of town, where his construction company was starting a new housing development.

The silence was broken when she showed him where to drop her off, and he pulled into the driveway. As soon as he turned the key to shut off the engine, she reached for the door handle and opened the door.

Running like a scared rabbit. If that's the way she felt, he was okay with it. He didn't have any intention of trying to change her mind or resurrect the past.

She slid from the seat and climbed out of the truck, then turned back. "Thank you, Nick. Tell Tony to send me a bill for the tire."

The door slammed shut, and he watched her cross the lawn and head for the porch. When she stepped up on the first porch step, his jacket slid from her shoulders. Before he could stop himself, he was out of the truck and replacing the coat around her.

Taking the box from her grasp, he tried for a smile. "You have your hands full."

She hesitated, and then turned to look at him, her gaze meeting his. "You always were a gentleman, Nick Morelli."

He didn't have the chance to read the look in her eyes when the storm door in front of them blew open.

"Mom! We thought you got lost."

"Mommy, I don't want to go to bed without you," came a cry from behind the small boy, who had burst from the house first.

Becca hurried up the steps to the door and knelt down to take the boy into her arms. "I wasn't lost, honey. I had a flat tire." She held out one arm and pulled a small, towheaded girl to her. "It's okay, April. I'm home and everything is all right."

The little boy pulled away a few inches and looked up at Nick. "Who's he?"

Becca swiveled and offered Nick an apologetic smile. "He's the nice man who stopped to help me with the flat tire."

"Where's our car?" the boy asked, his forehead creased in a worried frown.

The whimper of a baby caused Nick to look up to see Raylene Stevens holding an infant. "Nick brought you home?" she asked Becca, but didn't take her eyes off him. "It's good to see you, Nick."

"You, too, Raylene." He hadn't seen Becca's best friend since he'd left town ten years ago. The night was turning into a walk down memory lane, and he didn't want to go there. He sure hoped her strange smile didn't mean she thought he'd taken some kind of advantage of Becca.

"I found her out on one of the back roads with a flat and a spare that matched it," he explained in defense, adding a shrug. "I'll have Tony take care of it in the morning. He can drop her car off at her place after he fixes the tire."

Becca unwrapped the two kids still clinging to her and held her arms out for the baby. After planting a kiss on the baby's forehead, she turned to Nick. "Thank you for the ride and…everything. But don't bother Tony about the car. It really isn't necessary."

"I will and it is," he said, his gaze on the infant she cuddled. "Is this Daisy?"

"Yes, and I'd better get her inside and out of the cold before she gets worse."

He lifted his hand to run a finger down the soft skin of the baby's cheek. He had always had a soft spot for kids. "Get better, Daisy," he whispered. Ready to put an end to the bizarre night, he ruffled the boy's hair and handed the box to Raylene. "I'll tell Tony to get right on the tire, first thing," he told Becca. "Nice seeing both of you again." He turned, hurrying down the steps.

"Crazy," he muttered to himself as he backed his truck out of the driveway. Having Tony go after her car was nothing. He would've done it for anybody. Of course, he would make sure his brother sent her husband the bill.

His frown deepened. And where *was* Becca's husband? Why wasn't he out looking for his wife, when his children were obviously worried about her? Some guys just didn't know when they had it good.

But Becca's husband wasn't his worry. As soon as he knew her car was taken care of, he could go about his own business. Becca Malone was a thing of the past. And she would stay that way.

"I CAN'T BELIEVE IT was Nick Morelli who found you," Raylene said. "Of all people to run into."

Becca started to shush her, but with the kids settled in the Stevenses' family room, she didn't have to worry about little ears. She had a few choice words of her own about her run of bad luck—seeing Nick again topped the list— but she didn't share them. Instead, she checked to make sure Daisy's fever hadn't gotten any worse. She couldn't bear to see her baby hurting and sick. If only Daisy's father felt the same way.

"Becca?"

She turned to attempt a smile for her best friend. "I'm just glad somebody found me. I don't know how I would've gotten home if Nick hadn't stopped."

"So what do you think?"

"About what?" Becca gathered Daisy's blanket and stuffed it into the diaper bag, making a mental note that she couldn't put off doing laundry another day. If she had to hang clothes on the line in freezing weather because the house didn't include a dryer, that's all there was to it.

"About Nick being home, of course," Raylene chattered as she followed Becca out of the room.

Becca could have done without this little interrogation, but she and Raylene had been best friends since grade school. Raylene had been through it all with her, especially during the time she and Nick had dated, knowing every detail and lending support. Of course her friend was curious, and she deserved at least a simple answer.

"It was a surprise."

"A surprise?" Raylene stepped around Becca and faced her, bringing her to a halt. "A surprise? Is that all it was?"

"I had to take the back roads because of the road construction on the highway. Then the tire went flat. To be honest, I was surprised that anybody stopped or was even in the vicinity. So to answer your question, yes."

"But isn't 'surprised' putting it kind of mildly?"

Becca couldn't stop the wry grin. "Yes, I suppose it is. Shocked would be more like it."

Raylene laughed and flopped to the sofa. "'Shock' is a good word."

"What's he doing here?" Becca hoped her curiosity sounded normal.

"Whatever he wants, I suppose," her best friend said with a shrug. "And his wife isn't with him."

Becca's heart stopped beating for a brief moment. Chastising herself for being cheered by the news, she forced herself to breathe. "Maybe she's coming later."

"Could be. He's staying at his parents' house. That's all I know." She slid a sly look at Becca. "But I could find out."

Becca shook her head. "No, there's no reason to do that. Nick Morelli isn't interested in me. I blew that ten years ago."

"Your dad blew that for you ten years ago," Raylene reminded her. "If you'd had your way—"

"What's done is done. That was the past and this is the here and now."

"But don't you ever wonder what might have happened?"

Becca didn't bother to answer her. What good would wondering do? As far as Nick Morelli was concerned, their roles had switched. She had once been the daughter of one of the most influential men in town and was expected to marry well. Nick had been the son of a garage owner. A guy who pumped gas to earn his way through college. Not that it had made a difference to her, but it had to her father.

She had done what was expected of her. She had married the man her father had chosen for her, instead of going to college. But that hadn't turned out so well. Not after seven years of marriage and two children, with the third born barely a month before the divorce was final.

And Nick? From what she had heard, he had done wonderfully well. College graduate, owner of his own company and married to a Denver debutante.

Yes, she had wondered what might have happened had

she not done as her father had wanted her to do or if things had been different. She and Nick had dated for almost six months and had fallen in love. But it all changed a week before her high school graduation, when her father decided to put a stop to it. She hadn't given that part of her past a lot of thought, especially during the last few years. She had only had time to deal with what life dealt her and survive.

Right now, she didn't want to talk about Nick. In fact, she didn't want to think about him. "Where did you put Daisy's bottle?" she asked.

"It's in the kitchen," Raylene said, getting to her feet. "And I have an extra can of formula you can take home with you."

"Raylene, I can't—"

"No big deal," Raylene answered with a wave of her hand as she disappeared into the kitchen.

But it *was* a big deal. To Becca. Maybe she could convince Raylene to count it as a present. With Christmas a little more than three weeks away and less than a hundred dollars left to last until then, she couldn't turn down the offer. She was still trying to figure out how to buy groceries, pay bills and have enough to buy a few small gifts for Danny and April. And the rent was going to be late, if, as had happened too many times, the child support money didn't arrive.

Fighting the panic at the thought and reminding herself that she would get control of her life and make it better, she jumped at the sound of the doorbell.

"Get the door, will you?" Raylene called from the kitchen. "Jeff probably forgot his key again. And I want to fix another bottle for Daisy so you'll have it when you get home."

Glad for the chance to get her mind off her troubles, Becca went to the door and reached for the doorknob, ready to tease Jeff. Opening the door, she put on a sultry smile and batted her eyelashes. "Cash, check or credit card?"

"Depends."

She felt the heat flood her cheeks when she realized that it wasn't Jeff but Nick standing on the porch. "I thought you were… I mean, I was only…"

Nick smiled, and the heat from her cheeks spread throughout her body. Nick's smile was the same. Beautiful. And it left her breathless. One more thing she didn't have control of.

He looked past her, then back at her again. "I was hoping you hadn't gone."

She leaned against the door for support. "Raylene is in the kitchen and—"

"I forgot to ask where you live."

She blinked. "Where I live?"

"Yeah, so Tony can drop off your car tomorrow when he has the tire fixed. I suppose he knows, but just in case…"

Of course. Why else would he need to know that? But she didn't want him to go to the trouble. "There's really no need. I'll see if Jeff—"

"Here's Daisy's bottle. I'll just put it in— Oh!"

Becca turned to see Raylene. Moving away from the doorway, she opened the door wider. "I was just telling Nick that I'd see if Jeff could take my tire to get it fixed tomorrow," she explained.

"Not tomorrow," Raylene said, bending over to put the bottle in the diaper bag. "He has a dentist appointment. The last thing he'll want to do is change a tire." She straightened and made a face. "Knowing him, he'll spend the rest of the day zoned out on pain pills and insisting that he's dying."

"Who's dying?" a voice said from behind Nick.

Becca wanted to answer that *she* was. Nick brought back too many memories. And she wouldn't accept favors from him.

"Becca had a flat," Raylene explained as she moved to greet her husband.

Nick stepped back to let Jeff pass, and the two men exchanged greetings. "I found her on the side of the road about five miles from town," Nick explained when Jeff had given his wife a brief kiss. "I'll have Tony take care of it. No reason for you to do it. He can drop her car at her place when it's done."

"But—" Becca said, hoping to find another way.

"I told you it wasn't a problem," Nick insisted. "Tony has plenty of help."

"You'll have to take him up on the offer," Jeff said. "I have to go to the—"

"Dentist," Nick and Becca said in unison.

"All I need to know is where she lives," Nick went on, turning to look at her and obviously expecting an answer.

Becca had her reasons for not telling him. It would bring the past into the present. But in spite of that, it was clear that she couldn't refuse his offer, no matter how badly she wanted to.

"The old Watkins place," she said.

Nick was silent for a moment. "The old Watkins place?"

"Yes."

"The one west of town?"

"You remember where it is, don't you? About seven miles west on Morgan Creek Road. Or do you need directions?"

Nick shook his head. "Yeah. I mean, no, I don't need directions. I remember where it is."

While Raylene and Jeff excused themselves, Becca wondered what memories the area held for him. Were they the same as hers? Teenagers still took advantage of the double row of hedge trees on the road that ran past her house, providing seclusion for stolen kisses. And other things. She and Nick had spent more than a few nights there, before he had taken her home, talking, dreaming and…

"If it's too far—" she began, wishing the memories away.

"No. It's no trouble. I just— I didn't know you lived there. I thought you lived here in town. That's all."

He remembered. And she needed him not to know that she did, too. "It's nice sometimes not to have close neighbors," she said, trying for a smile. "There's more…privacy."

"Yeah, I guess there is." He stood looking at her for a moment, and then reached into his pocket. "Do you need the key to your house?"

"Oh! I'd forgotten you had it with the car key. But Raylene has an extra. She can let me in."

"Okay, then." He shifted from one foot to the other, as if he had something else to say. "I'll make sure Tony gets the tire fixed first thing in the morning. You might need to go somewhere."

"Thank you."

"Sure. Good night."

"Good night, Nick."

She watched as he turned and started down the steps. He was almost to his truck when she remembered his jacket. "Wait!" she called to him. "You forgot something." She ran to grab his jacket from a chair in the kitchen and hurried outside with it.

Nick sat waiting in his truck with the motor running.

When she reached it, he rolled down his window. "You'll need it on the way home tonight," he said when she held it out to him. "Give it to Tony or whoever brings your car back tomorrow."

Sensing that it wouldn't do any good to argue, she nodded. As she watched him back out of the driveway, she shivered and quickly reminded herself that the past was over. And Nick Morelli didn't have a place in her present— or her future.

Chapter Two

Nick gathered what patience he had left, while his brother finished the oil change on Becca's car. "Why didn't you tell me?"

Lowering the hood of the older model Lexus, which had seen better days, Tony looked up at him. "I figured you knew."

"No. How could I?" He hadn't had much sleep the night before. Learning that Becca was living in the old Watkins place had been a blow. The old Victorian house had always been a favorite of his. Since he was a kid, he had wanted it for his own, but he'd never dreamed it ever would be. Not even when he had shared his dream with Becca, all those years ago.

When the opportunity to buy the house from Mrs. Watkins had presented itself three months ago, in the midst of his decision to move his construction company from Denver to Katyville, he'd jumped at the chance. She had told him there was someone living there, and he'd had his attorney take the necessary legal steps to remedy the situation and keep the transaction anonymous by sending a notice to vacate under his corporate name to the tenant. He'd been generous, giving the tenant more than the usual amount of time to move before he would start the planned renovations on the house.

Had planned.

"She's all ready, Nick."

Nick jerked his head up to see Tony wiping his hands on a rag. "Send the bill to her husband," he said and turned to leave.

"Becca's husband? I don't know— Hey! Where are you going?"

"I have work to do," Nick called to him from halfway across the garage. "Have Mike deliver it as soon as he can."

Running into Becca the night before had been a surprise he could have done without. Now that he knew her car had been taken care of, he could get back to feeling guilty about making her move with a sick baby, as if that was something he had anything to do with and as if he didn't need to be overseeing the transition of his construction company.

"Mike is gone today," Tony called after him. "And Travis won't be here for another twenty minutes. You'll have to take it yourself."

Halfway to the bay door, Nick stopped and looked back. "Not me."

Tony gave him a slow grin. "She still getting under your skin?"

"You're crazy," Nick replied and continued on his way.

"She won't have a car if you don't take it to her."

Nick gritted his teeth. The last thing he wanted to do was see Becca again. He hadn't been able to forget the come-hither look in her eyes or her sexy pout when she'd opened Raylene's door the night before. Even knowing it hadn't been for him and was only a joke, the thought of it still did things to him he didn't like happening.

"Nick, she and her husband—"

"Okay!" He took a deep breath. "Okay. I'll take her car out there and Travis can pick me up as soon as he gets here."

Fifteen minutes later, after enduring Tony's devilish grin while he backed the car out of the garage bay, Nick slowed Becca's car as he approached her house. *His* house, he reminded himself, looking for signs of life. He had driven by once to check out the house since he'd returned to Katyville, but hadn't seen anyone outside. Too busy adjusting to the slower pace of small-town life and getting his company set up, he hadn't inquired about his tenants. He hadn't cared, knowing his attorney had taken care of everything. But it hadn't been taken care of, he reminded himself. Not yet, anyway.

Determined to get this over with as soon as possible, Nick parked the car in the gravel driveway and got out, concentrating on the house and what would need to be done before he could start the renovations to bring it back to its once-glorious condition.

After a quick rap on the door, he waited, prepared to face Becca and uneasy about bringing up the subject of his ownership of the house.

The door swung open to reveal the little blond girl he had seen the night before. The spitting image of her mother, right down to the green eyes, she stood silently staring at him.

"Is your mom home?" he asked.

Her fingertip went straight to her mouth, and her wide-eyed innocence made him smile. She shook her head, sending the short, sassy ponytail she wore dancing back and forth.

He looked past her to see her older brother standing in the entryway, studying him.

"You're the guy who helped Mom with the car last night."

Nick nodded. "And I've brought her car back, all fixed again."

The boy's serious expression didn't change. "Thanks." But he seemed to be struggling with something. "My name's Danny and this is April."

"And I'm Nick. Nice to meet you both. And you're welcome." Not only had he had the flat fixed and the slow leak in the spare taken care of, but he'd also added a minor tune-up to the work order. He figured that if her husband didn't have the sense to have it done, the guy deserved to be surprised with the bill for the work.

"Mom's in the backyard."

Wishing for a chance to look around inside the house, Nick thanked him, deciding it would be best to curb his curiosity until Becca knew he was now the owner. Until then, she might not appreciate him poking around.

"I can show you where," the boy said.

"No, that's okay. I think I can manage. And she knows I was bringing her car."

The boy gave a stiff nod. "Close the door, April," he told his sister.

Nick grinned as he stood staring at a door that had closed much quicker than it had opened. It was pretty clear the boy was leery of strangers. And protective of his mother.

As he walked down the steps of the broad, wraparound porch, Nick made a mental note of the repairs and materials he would need, once he could start work.

But something wasn't right. If her husband was a stockbroker, the condition of the house sure didn't show that he had spent time thinking about upkeep. Of course, some renters didn't feel they needed to bother with it, and considered it the landlord's responsibility. But what he really wanted to know was why the hell they were renting, not living in some fancy new house. And why this place?

His first reaction the night before when he had learned Becca was living here was that he would tear it down. But he had instantly known he wouldn't let her ruin his dream. By now, Becca and her hotshot husband should have received the letter explaining the sale and the date they were to vacate. Although she hadn't mentioned anything about moving, and he wondered why. Did she remember the plans they had made? But she couldn't, not and live there now with her husband. She couldn't be that heartless.

Or could she? After all, it had been ten years and—

When he turned the corner at the back of the house, he saw Becca, bringing him up short and reminding him that he would have to tell her exactly who he was—the man evicting her family.

BECCA BLEW ON HER nearly numb fingers and wished, once again, that Katyville had a Laundromat where she could sit back and read a book while her laundry tumbled until it was too hot to touch.

"There you are. I was looking for you."

Startled by Nick's voice, Becca dropped the shirt she was attempting to hang on the clothesline. *Darn it, anyway.* It figured he would show up at the worst time. Again.

His long strides brought him across the barren backyard, and he bent to retrieve the shirt from the ground. "Don't you think this is taking fresh-smelling clothes a bit too far?" he asked, grabbing her hand and examining her fingers.

Snatching her hand away, she hid it and the other behind her back. "How would you know about fresh-smelling clothes?"

"You must've forgotten my Italian mother," he answered.

Seeing that he was about as out-of-the-loop as anyone could be, she didn't bother to tell him that she knew his mother well.

And then she did the unforgivable. She looked up and met his gaze.

His sexy, lopsided grin was all too familiar. She wished he would go away, back to Denver or *anywhere* besides her backyard. At least he hadn't reminded her that the old Becca wouldn't have been caught dead hanging clothes on a line outside, even in the best of weather.

As if he could read her thoughts, he broke the gaze holding hers. "Your car's in the driveway," he told her, picking two clothespins from the bag and hanging the shirt.

"You don't need to do that." She had the urge to shove him aside, but she knew that physical contact with him would be her undoing, so she pulled out one of Danny's T-shirts instead and attempted to fasten it to the line with cold, trembling fingers. "And thank you for taking care of my car."

He took a step back and crossed his arms on his broad chest, leveling his gaze on her. "How's Daisy this morning? Any better?"

"Much better," she answered. The baby's fever had broken during the night, and she was breathing easier. Both of them were. There would be no trip to the emergency room this time.

He said nothing else while she finished hanging the few remaining items. When she bent to pick up the empty basket and bag of pins, he stepped forward and took them from her.

She gave him a quick smile to thank him, realizing that he wasn't leaving immediately. "Isn't someone here to take you back?"

"Travis should be here any minute," he said as they walked to the house.

Just having him near set her pulse to racing, but she tried to ignore it as they stopped on the small porch leading to the back door. "There's coffee left. Would you like a cup while you wait?"

Nick hesitated. "I'll wait in your car, if that's okay. It shouldn't be long. Besides, I wouldn't want anyone to get the wrong idea if I went inside with you."

"Anyone?" she asked, puzzled at his scowl.

"You know, like the neighbors or…your husband."

She knew she should tell him the truth, but she hesitated to do it. Of course, it wouldn't make any difference to him, but she didn't want him thinking she was a hot divorcée looking for a new man. "Still worried about gossip?" she asked, her hand on the doorknob.

"You were the one who had the problem with gossip."

She knew it probably had seemed that way to him, but it had been more her father's problem than hers. "I guess so," she said, knowing better. "Living here, outside of Katyville, has made me immune to it."

"But I'm not immune to an angry husband who might decide to take a poke at me for drinking coffee with his wife. No matter how innocent it might be."

Struggling with whether to be truthful or not, she opened the door and set the basket and bag of clothespins he handed her inside. Turning back to him, she knew she had to and wondered how to answer. If she told him the truth, would he think it was an invitation? But if she didn't, he was bound to find out and wonder why she hadn't said anything. She had only lied once, and that was to him, ten years ago. This time, she owed it to him to be honest.

"There's no husband, angry or otherwise."

His scowl deepened. "But I thought—"

She shook her head, not knowing what else to say and definitely not wanting to go in to the details. Standing half-inside the door, she waited for him to say something.

"You'd better get inside and get that door closed," he finally answered. "I'll wait here or in the car."

Relieved and disappointed at the same time, she didn't fail to notice that he had already taken a couple of steps off the porch. "Thanks," she said, not knowing what else to say. "And tell Tony I'll pay for the tire repair soon."

"Like I said last night, it's on the house." Either that or he would pay it. He took a few more steps away and made it to the corner of the house. "Well, nice seeing you again, Becca."

"You, too, Nick," she said, but he had already disappeared.

Taking a deep breath, she let herself inside. As she moved the empty basket to a corner, she pushed all thoughts of Nick from her mind. There were more important things to think about.

The sounds of cartoon characters coming from the television in the living room assured her that Danny and April were occupied, at least for a few minutes. She'd found some cold medicine and given it to Daisy only an hour ago, so she was sure the baby would sleep for a while.

Reaching into a kitchen drawer, she took an envelope and a pad of paper from under the local phone book. The old kitchen chair scraped the linoleum when she pulled it away from the table.

"There has to be a way," she whispered as she sat and removed the legal-looking document from the envelope. If she couldn't find an answer, she and the kids would have nowhere to live. She needed to get control of her life. She needed just a little good news, a little break. Now.

NICK DRUMMED his fingers on the steering wheel, as he waited in Becca's car for his ride back to the garage, his anger building by the minute. For as long as he could remember, his mother had scolded him daily for his hot, Italian temper. But, dammit, why the hell hadn't Tony told him Becca was divorced? Why hadn't his mother? She had told him everything else that had happened in Katyville during his absence.

He couldn't believe his luck. He was on the verge of making a dream come true. All he needed was the old Watkins place. And it was his. *His.* But he couldn't very well throw Becca and her kids out. Nobody had to tell him that she was struggling. How that could be, he didn't know. If her stockbroker husband wasn't paying the correct child support and alimony, surely her father would. It wasn't *his* job to do it. Why should he care about her? She had made it clear ten years ago that she didn't have any feelings or use for him.

But he really didn't have a choice. If and when his mother got wind of any of this, there'd be hell to pay. He hadn't mentioned the old Watkins place to any of his family, except Tony, and he was sure his brother hadn't said anything.

His frustration hadn't eased any after waiting twenty

minutes for a ride back to the garage. Where was Travis? Clouds had rolled in and the day was getting colder. Nick pulled his jacket closer, refusing to turn on the engine to run the heater.

Getting colder and grumpier by the minute, he finally gave in and walked to the house. He had hoped he wouldn't have to see Becca until he had a plan mapped out for telling her he was her new landlord, but he for damned sure wasn't going to freeze in the process.

This time Becca answered his knock. "I don't know how to thank you," she told him when he handed her the car keys. She looked past him. "Do you need me to take you back to town? I mean, I don't see anyone…"

He stuffed his hands in his jacket pockets. "I was wondering if I could use your phone to call Tony. I forgot my cell phone."

"Of course," she said, opening the door wider to let him in.

"And I wouldn't mind that cup of coffee you offered earlier. If you still have some."

"In the kitchen. I just made a fresh pot."

As he followed her through the house, he took the opportunity to get a closer view of what would need to be done to the interior, once he could start on the renovations. From what he could see, the house was in excellent structural shape. Much better than he had hoped, considering he doubted Mrs. Watkins had bothered with many repairs after her husband died.

"The phone's over there." Becca pointed to the phone on the kitchen wall.

While she poured coffee and set the filled cups on the

table, he punched in the number for the garage. After several rings, Tony answered. Nick had to bite his tongue to keep from shouting at him.

"I thought you were going to pick me up," he said, as calmly as he could.

"Something came up. Look, Nick, it's going to be a while."

Nick could hear Travis talking in the background, and the voice of what he assumed was a customer. Neither sounded all that happy. "How long? Any idea?"

"Half an hour. No more. Stan Perkins is leaving on a business trip, so we don't have any more time than that."

Nick hadn't been prepared to spend more than fifteen minutes in Becca's company, but he didn't have a choice. "I'll see you in forty-five minutes then," he told Tony and hung up.

"Trouble?" Becca asked.

"Tony had an emergency come up, so it looks like you'll have to put up with me a little longer."

"Oh." Twin lines appeared between her eyes. "I can always run you back to town," she said with little enthusiasm. "The kids are down for naps right now. Not that Danny takes one, but…"

It was clear to Nick that she didn't consider him being there a lucky break. "Don't wake the kids," he insisted. "If I'm in the way, maybe I can—"

He had a sudden thought. He was here, in his house, with the opportunity to do some poking around. This wasn't the time to tell her the truth. He would, though. Soon. But he *could* take advantage of the situation and maybe make having him around a little easier for her. "Would you mind if I look around? This old place always intrigued me as a kid."

Her worried frown deepened, but was quickly replaced with a soft smile. "It is something special, isn't it? I hate the thought of—" Her eyes clouded for a moment and she shook her head.

Was she remembering? Or thinking about having to leave it?

But she smiled again, even though it was weak. "I'll give you a quick tour and show you where the best things are, if you want me to. Then you can wander all you want."

For Nick, it was the perfect suggestion, although he didn't see the need for the tour. "Sounds good to me. Lead the way."

"We'll start here in the kitchen," she said, her cheeks coloring with pink. "I guess that's pretty easy to figure out."

As she pointed out some of the things that would be considered unusual for a newer house, Nick noticed that she relaxed. By the time they reached the stairs and she was showing him the hidden storage space under the staircase, he had made several mental notes about things he hadn't been aware of.

"I've been in here before," he told her.

She turned to look at him. "Really? When?"

Apparently she didn't remember that he had told her the story when they were younger. Relieved, he looked over his shoulder, pretending to make sure no one was listening. "You won't tell anyone, will you?"

She shook her head, her green eyes sparkling with mischief.

"Well," he said, lowering his voice to a more intimate level, "when I was about nine years old, Corey Jacobs and I walked out here from town one night and pried open a window."

Her gasp ended with a smothered, girlish giggle. "Didn't anybody catch you? I mean, somebody would have heard you, wouldn't they?"

"Mr. and Mrs. Watkins were away. I knew they would be because they'd had their car tuned up for a long road trip." He smiled, remembering how scared he and Corey had been that someone would drive by and see the light from their flashlights inside the house. "Of course, it was different than it is now. They had some pretty old-fashioned furnishings in here. And the floors creak more now than they did then. But that's easy to fix."

Becca leaned against the wall and sighed. "I like those old creaks. I remember when Mr. Watkins was still alive and the two of them would come into town. He was such a gentleman. But even then, she was a crotchety old thing. I never could understand how the two of them managed to stay married for so long. But I guess opposites attract."

Nick nodded, seeing the couple in his mind as they had been in his childhood. "Bill Watkins was a fine man. My dad always said he had the patience of a saint."

Becca laughed softly. "My mom used to say Vera Watkins had the tongue of a serpent."

But her laugh quickly faded. Nick wished it back again, but quickly chided himself. Whether Becca Malone was happy or not didn't change anything for him. But he couldn't help hoping to see another smile. Before he could think of something to say, he heard the phone ring.

"Go on upstairs," she told him. "If you're quiet, you won't wake the kids. They're used to me coming and going during nap time."

She disappeared into the kitchen to answer the phone,

and he quickly pulled out a notebook from his back pocket
that held his notes for the house. He was constantly
thinking of things he wanted to do to with the place when
the time came that he could. Seeing it up close again, he
knew nothing could make him destroy it, not even the
memories of sharing his dream with Becca.

There were a number of repairs that needed to be made.
In several places, some of the decorative molding at the
ceiling had been damaged and would need fixing or replacing. And Becca might like the creaky floors, but to Nick that
meant there might be some warping. At least from what he
could tell, nothing had caused them to slant from settling over
the years. The foundation was obviously in very good shape.

He was curious about the heating and started for the
kitchen to ask Becca if she would mind if he took a look
at the furnace, but as he approached the doorway into the
room, he could hear her side of the phone conversation.

"Yes, I know it's due the first of the month—today,
Mrs. Watkins," she was saying. "And I know I'll have to
pay a penalty for being late…again… Yes, I know we don't
have much time left before we have to leave. I have your
letter and the notice to vacate right here…. I hope to have
the money to you by the end of next week, at the latest.
Perhaps if you'd give me the name of the new owner,
maybe I could… Yes, I understand…goodbye."

Nick wasn't sure whether to walk in as if he hadn't
heard a thing or whether to try to make it back to the stairs
before she reappeared. He heard the sound of papers being
shuffled and then a sniff. A sliver of guilt gnawed at him,
but he didn't get a chance to deal with it. Becca came out
of the kitchen with her head down and ran into him.

His arms instinctively went around her to steady her when they collided. It was the wrong thing to do.

"I—I'm so sorry," she blurted, attempting to take a step back, but unable to do so as he held her. "I have…I've had some bad news."

Torn by a sudden urge to comfort her, but knowing it would only make matters worse, Nick released her. Stepping back, he did his best to ignore the glitter of tears in her eyes. "Do you want to talk about it?" he dared to ask.

"Yes. I mean, no." She turned around, hiding her face. Her drooping shoulders lifted, and then squared as she took a deep breath. When she faced him again, there were no tears glistening in her eyes, and she wore a weak smile. "I'm sorry, Nick. It isn't something I feel comfortable talking about right now. Suffice it to say that Mrs. Watkins is no longer my landlady. This place has just been sold."

He swallowed. Hard. Here was his opportunity to tell her the truth. But he couldn't. He'd freeze, walking back to town, and she'd have to be a saint not to toss him out the door, if he told her. Not to mention that he couldn't add to her misery. Not right now.

Becca shook her head and walked into the living room, while Nick followed. "I never would have thought she would sell this house. I didn't know she was even thinking about doing it. In fact, I thought she was happy I'd rented it—it stood empty for a long time after she moved into Katyville. And now she's sold it to some corporation. I don't know why. Maybe she needed the extra income. I still pay my rent to her, but she just told me that she forwards it on to the new owner. Or owners. I suspect they'll tear it down."

A tiny prick of guilt stabbed at him. Hadn't he thought of doing just that? He opened his mouth to tell her that wouldn't happen and instantly shut it. He couldn't let on that he knew anything about this. Saying nothing would be best, until he was prepared to tell her the truth. Lying wasn't something he did, as a rule. His parents had taught him that truth was always the best option, and the consequences for not telling it would be a lot worse than what the truth would get him. He knew he would have to deal with the consequences of this later. When the time was right—and it definitely wasn't right at the moment—he would find a way to tell her.

"So what does that mean for you? And the kids?" he asked, hoping she had found another place to live by now.

Sinking to the sofa, she hung her head, her hands tightly clasped in her lap. "It means we have to leave. We have until the first Monday after the New Year to pack and find a new home."

"A little over a month then." An easy thing for him to say, since he'd been counting down the time when the house would be empty. "Where will you move?"

She shook her head, her lips set in a thin line.

"You don't know?" he asked in disbelief.

She shook her head again.

He felt like the world's biggest jerk. He didn't need the extra money, but because he preferred that the sale remain anonymous until he was ready to make it known, his lawyer had suggested that the rent continue to be sent to Mrs. Watkins, who would then send it to his attorney for deposit. He sure hadn't counted on the tenant being someone he knew, let alone *Becca*. In fact, he had been in such a rush to close the deal, and so busy making arrangements to move his very lucrative construction company to Katyville, he had left everything up to his attorney.

"I don't mean to whine to you," she said, her voice quivering. "But you did ask." She sniffed again, and then looked up at him with a watery smile. "I truly am sorry."

"Don't worry about it." *Right.* He'd worry about it enough for the both of them.

"If only we had until spring."

But by spring, Nick hoped to have most of the interior repairs done and be ready to start on the outside. He hadn't taken into consideration that a single mother and her three kids might be homeless because of his dream. Knowing it was Becca didn't make it easier, no matter what she had done to him in the past. Helping her sure wasn't a part of his plan—until now.

"Somebody's here!" Danny shouted from upstairs, relieving Nick from commenting or having to make any rash decisions.

"It must be Travis," Nick said, more than ready to leave.

After thanking her for the coffee and the tour of the house, he said goodbye and hurried outside to the waiting truck.

Climbing in, he slammed the door. "I have *you* to thank for this mess I'm in."

Tony looked at him. "I learned a long time ago to mind my own business, so don't blame your troubles on me."

Nick realized he was being unreasonable and let out a long sigh. "You should've told me Becca was single again."

Putting the truck in gear, Tony grunted. "Why? It wouldn't have made any difference."

Nick considered it and wasn't sure his brother wasn't right. Over the past ten years, he hadn't grown any fonder of Becca. Not that he hadn't thought of her. But he had always resented the way she had so casually dumped him. By the time he heard she had married, he wasn't in the mood to wish her well. After that, he did his best to forget her. And now this had happened.

"At least I would've known what I was up against," he managed to reply.

"Nick, the thorough planner," Tony replied with a touch of disgust, as he backed the truck down the drive and onto the road.

"It's worked well to this point."

"Yeah? What about—" Tony pressed his lips together and shook his head.

Nick knew he was thinking of Edie, his ex-wife. "There are some things you can't plan for," he said.

Tony avoided looking at him as they headed for Katyville. "So what do you do when something like that happens?"

Nick shrugged, thinking of how he had handled what he called the bumps in the road. "Regroup. Find another way." And that was exactly what he would do now.

Chapter Three

"Mom?"

Becca turned from the window where she had been watching Nick climb into Tony's truck. "Rest time isn't over yet, Danny."

He scrunched up his face and shrugged. "But I need to ask you something."

Taking him by the hand, she led him to the sofa and pulled him onto her lap. "What is it, honey?"

"That…that man that brought you to Raylene's last night…"

"Nick," she prompted with a nod.

"Yeah, him. Well, you know, you always told us never to talk to strangers and I know you had to when he stopped to help you with the car, but isn't that kinda danger…dangerous?"

Becca smiled. He was far too wise for his five years. From the moment his dad had left them, Danny had been her protector. The man of the house. He never stopped looking out for her and his sisters.

"You don't have to worry," she told him, brushing his hair away from his eyes. "Nick isn't a stranger. I knew him a long, long time ago, when I was young."

Danny tipped his head up and looked at her, his blue eyes serious. "You're not old, Mom."

She couldn't stop the laugh that bubbled up inside her. "Okay. When I was younger. How's that?"

For a moment, he didn't say anything. When he looked at her again, she couldn't read his expression. "Do you…" He ducked his head.

"Do I what?"

He took a deep breath, let it out slowly, then looked up at her. "Do you like him?"

Completely taken by surprise, Becca wasn't sure how to answer. "Like him?" she repeated. "He's a friend, I guess. Is that what you mean?"

His lips curved up in a mischievous smile. "Sort of."

"Now, Danny—"

"It's okay, Mom. I just wanted to make sure he was okay, that's all. And if he wants to come around, that's okay, too."

"Oh, really?" She had to bite the inside of her cheek to keep from laughing. Or maybe it was to keep from crying. She wasn't sure which. There was no reason for Nick to come around again. In fact, she hoped he wouldn't. He couldn't do anything to help her, even if he wanted to, and she was pretty sure he didn't. He really, really didn't understand her situation. While it was true that he hadn't had the advantages she'd had growing up, she doubted he had ever lived in fear of losing his home or worrying about how to feed his family. But for her—

The phone rang, and Danny jumped from her lap, shouting, "I'll get it!" as he ran to the kitchen. Becca hoped it wasn't Mrs. Watkins calling to hassle her for the rent money again.

Danny poked his head through the doorway. "It's Grandpa," he announced with a sour expression.

Becca's heart stopped momentarily, but revived instantly to beat a heavy thud. Her father rarely called, so it must be important. She took the phone from her son and covered the mouthpiece. "Go check on your sisters for me, will you?"

As soon as he was out of the room, she put the receiver to her ear. "Hello, Daddy. What a surprise to hear from you."

"Surprise? Why would you be surprised after sending a request for money?"

She bit back the threatening groan. She had completely forgotten, in a moment of madness, that she had written her father and asked for some help with the rent. "Oh, that."

"Yes, *that*," he grumbled. "Do you think I have money to throw away?"

Bristling at the inference that a small loan from him would compare to wasting money, she quickly and silently counted to ten. "Don't worry about it."

"I'm not losing any sleep, that's for sure. If you'd been the wife you should've been to Jason, you wouldn't be doing without."

If only her father had really known the man he had chosen for her, he wouldn't have the nerve to say the things he said. But there was no sense telling her father that. As always, he was right and she was wrong. "It really doesn't matter, Daddy. It's a done deal now. I just found myself a little pinched for money, that's all."

She'd found herself a *lot* pinched for money. The child support Jason was ordered to pay was always late and often not the full amount, *when* he even bothered to pay it. For the most part, when he did, it kept the four of them fed and a roof over their heads, but little more. She had been looking for work, but she hadn't found anything just yet.

"So how are things down under?" she asked, changing the subject. Discussion of Jason would always be to his advantage and never to hers.

"It's hot, and Cecily is waiting for me to join her on the beach. Before I forget, look for some Christmas gifts in the mail for your kids. Ceci picked them out. I don't have any idea what would suit them."

You would if you took the time to know them. But she couldn't come right out and say that to him. No matter how far away he was now, he still had a measure of control over her, so she thanked him instead. "I'm sure they'll enjoy whatever you've sent," she added.

When the brief conversation ended, Becca leaned against the wall next to the phone and closed her eyes. The house was peacefully silent. She suspected all was well with the girls and Danny had found something to immerse himself in. She tried so hard to keep a happy face in front of her children, but some days were harder than others.

Opening her eyes, the first thing she saw was the coffee cup Nick had used. The sight of it spurred her into action. She wasn't going to think about Nick. She wasn't going to worry about the rent, the bills, or moving. She had things to do. There was laundry to finish and the boxes in her trunk to bring in. These were the things she could control. Daisy and April would be waking up soon, and once that happened, she wouldn't have time for feeling sorry for herself.

As she started to work, she flipped on the television to

catch the noon news, expecting to hear something about the comet she had seen the night before. To her dismay, there was nothing mentioned. By the time the program was over, her family was awake and clamoring for her attention.

After fixing lunch and entertaining them with a game of hide-and-seek, she was exhausted, but her chores weren't done. Standing in the laundry room, she watched the water inch its way across the old linoleum floor, while the washer did nothing. No agitator gyrating from side to side. No hum of the wash getting clean. Nothing happening but that steady, slow trickle of water.

"Looks like you have a problem."

She jumped at the sound of the voice and turned, surprised to see Nick.

"Danny let me in," he explained. "Tony forgot to put the stroller back in the trunk, so I told him I'd drop it off. I left it on the porch."

"You didn't need to do that."

"I was out, anyway," he said with a shrug. Reaching into his pocket, he pulled out a folded paper and handed it to her. "My sister moved this summer and kept the list she'd made of possible rentals. I thought it would save you some time."

"Thanks." She scanned the well-compiled list, wondering how she was supposed to come up with a deposit, when she couldn't even come up with enough for one month's rent. "Ann-Marie always was an organized person."

"My sister is a pack rat."

"Yes, but an organized pack rat. It makes a difference," she told him with a smile. She knew all of his family well.

He stared at her, their gazes locking until he finally looked away. Becca felt the warmth flow through her body and wished he would go away. She didn't need him here, bringing lists that were of no use to her and looks that threatened to melt her on the spot.

"Want me to take a look at that?" he asked, indicating the washing machine with a nod.

Becca wasn't sure she wanted to be beholden to him any more than she already was, but they needed clean clothes. "Do you know anything about washers?"

"Enough to know if they can be fixed or not."

She couldn't be sure if he was serious, but once again she wasn't in a position to refuse him. "I guess that's better than nothing and a lot more than I know. What can I do to help?"

He was already reaching behind the machine to turn off the water. "There's a toolbox out in the back of my truck. If you'd get it, I'll see what I can do here."

Relieved to escape, Becca grabbed her jacket and scooted out the door. The wind had picked up, blowing dirt and swirling around her legs, chilling her to the bone. Hurrying to his truck, she noticed the company logo on the side and came to a halt.

"Big Sky Construction," she whispered, staring at the graphic of stars, complete with a comet that looked like the twin of the one she had seen. She hadn't noticed it the night before. But then she had been in a state of shock at seeing Nick.

In the bed of the pickup truck, she found a red metal toolbox, but when she tried to pick it up, she could barely lift it. Putting all her effort into it, she finally managed to slide it to the edge of the tailgate and dragged it off, nearly smashing her toes in the process. She took a deep breath and squatted the way she had seen weight lifters on TV lift hundreds of pounds, and was finally able to pick it up from the ground. The distance to the house seemed like miles. She carried it with both hands gripping the handle, convinced her arms would be several inches longer. *If* she ever made it inside, she thought with a grimace of pain.

Getting up the back porch steps was the hardest part, and she kicked at the door, hoping someone would open it for her.

"Stay back," she puffed in warning, when the door opened to two small, curious faces. Danny and April made a wide berth for her as she struggled with the last few steps into the tiny laundry room. The box landed with a loud thud less than a foot behind Nick. Bent down and looking at the workings of the machine, he jumped back and nearly knocked her over.

"I'm sorry," she said when he turned to frown at her. "It was a little on the heavy side."

He looked at the toolbox and then at her, frowning. "No, I should be the one apologizing. I didn't think about how heavy it is."

With one hand, she massaged the muscles in her other arm. "And I thought my kids were heavy to carry around," she said, attempting a weak laugh.

Taking a step forward, he rubbed her arms. "Are you okay?"

"I'm fine." But she wasn't, especially when he stopped rubbing but didn't move his hands from her arms. She took a step to back up, and he jerked away as if he'd been burned. She watched as he opened the toolbox and dug through it, not sure if she should stay or go. "Can I do anything else to help?"

His hand stilled on a wrench. "Another cup of coffee would be nice."

There was a strange quality to his voice, and he didn't look at her as he went straight to the back of the machine without a glance. She didn't know how, but she was pretty certain she had made him mad.

"I'll fix a fresh pot," she said, then hurried out of the laundry room.

Glad to escape again, she tried to ignore the fact that Nick was less than ten feet away. She wasn't successful. The sounds of him moving around were a constant reminder. While he worked, she prayed that the machine would be simple to fix and that Nick would be gone soon. She didn't seem to be able to do or say anything right when he was around.

NICK LET OUT the breath he was holding when he was sure Becca was safely out of the room. What had he been thinking, sending her out to get his toolbox? Oh, he knew what he'd been thinking. And it wasn't the kind of thoughts he wanted to be having, and the reason he had sent her on the errand. But even now, with the challenge of fixing the washing machine on his mind, he still couldn't stop thinking about her. He could hear her running water in the kitchen. He could hear her moving, and he could imagine watching her. Becca looked even better than he had remembered. Still on the slender side, her body had rounded and softened. The kind of body men dreamed of holding and touch—

"Ouch!"

"Are you all right?" she called from the kitchen.

"Just great," he said, trying not to grit his teeth at the

pain in his smashed finger. If he didn't get his mind on what he was doing, he'd be a mangled mess before he could ever get the damned machine working again.

After forcing himself to concentrate on the task at hand, he was deep into the internal workings of the washer when he chanced to look up. Becca's son stood silently watching him. Nick leaned back against the wall, needing a break. Washing machines weren't his specialty, and it had been a while since he had watched his dad repair the family's washer.

"Can you fix it?" the boy asked, his expression too solemn for someone his size.

Nick was going more on hope than memory. "I think so. Might take a little time, though." When the boy continued to study him, Nick shifted his position. "You don't mind, do you?"

The boy shook his head, but didn't move from the spot.

Nick gestured for him to move closer. "Ever see the motor of one of these things?"

"No."

"Pretty simple," Nick said. Picking up a screwdriver, he kept talking, pointing out some of the parts he could name. As he talked, the boy moved closer, and he could remember himself at the same age. He had thought his father knew everything there was to know about anything. Still did, sometimes, even though he knew it wasn't true. He had a good relationship with his father and couldn't imagine what it would have been like not to have had him around when he was a kid.

"Do you like machines?" Nick asked.

"I guess."

Nick didn't miss the shrug of his small shoulders. "Yeah, I feel the same way. Now, my brother Tony really likes them. But me? I like wood."

"Wood?"

Keeping his attention on the work, Nick kept talking. "Yeah, like building things. You know. I like the feel of it in my hands. Sometimes it can be rough, sometimes as smooth as a baby's bu— Uh, skin. There's a lot you can do with wood."

"I made a birdhouse once," the boy said, hunkering down beside him. "It wasn't very good, though."

"Did you like making it?"

He nodded.

"Then that's what matters. As long as you enjoyed yourself."

"My dad never made things."

Nick's chest tightened at the face so devoid of emotion and wondered why the boy had used the past tense. Hadn't Becca's ex-husband been a good dad? Didn't he spend time with the boy now? Nick couldn't imagine any man not wanting to spend time with his son. Even though his own dad had spent hours at the garage, there had always been time for his sons. And daughters. But as much as Nick wanted to know more about Becca's ex-husband and what was happening, it wasn't his place to ask. Or to judge. "Not everybody likes it."

"Danny?"

Nick looked up to see Becca standing in the doorway, Daisy on her hip.

"You aren't bothering Nick, are you?" She looked from one to the other, her worry obvious.

"He's helping." Nick got to his feet and turned on the water faucets. "Give it a try, Danny."

The boy stood on tiptoe to reach the dial and pushed it in. They watched as the tub filled, then the motor kicked in and began agitating.

"It works!" Danny shouted.

Even Nick was somewhat surprised at his handiwork. "Want to give me a hand putting the back panel on?" he asked the boy.

"Can I?"

The joy on Danny's face was almost too much for Nick. Hadn't Mr. Stockbroker ever fixed anything? He handed Danny the screwdriver. "Help me line up the holes. When I get the screws slipped in, you screw 'em in tight, okay?"

Danny's head bobbed up and down.

Nick looked to see how Becca was reacting, but she was gone. He was sorry that she was missing how well Danny was doing. Spending this time with the boy had gotten his mind off the boy's mother. And Nick was more than grateful for that.

When they had finished the repair job, Danny insisted on helping Nick put the tools away. With one hand on the boy's shoulder and the other carrying the toolbox, Nick walked into the kitchen with Danny.

"We'll have to do this again sometime," Nick said, thinking of the renovations he would soon be doing. Maybe Becca would let him borrow Danny. Then again, maybe not. Not after she learned the truth.

"Would you like to stay for supper?" Becca turned from stirring a pot on the stove. "It isn't much. Stew, actually, but there's plenty of it."

She looked so pretty, with her face flushed from the heat of the stove, that Nick was nearly struck speechless. "Well, uh, it smells good, but I need to get going," he finally managed to say.

"My mom's a good cook," Danny said proudly.

Nick ruffled the boy's hair, but didn't take his eyes off Becca. "I'll bet she is."

"He's prejudiced," she said.

When Danny slipped away, Becca and the aroma of the food she was cooking drew Nick to take the few steps that brought him to stand directly behind her. Peering over her shoulder, he breathed in. "Sure smells good."

"The invitation is still open," she said without turning.

But Nick wasn't thinking only about the food. Becca smelled even better than the stew she was stirring. It wouldn't take much to imagine what a happy little domestic scene this could be. He could see himself after a hard day's work, stepping closer and slipping his arms around her. He'd pull her next to him. She'd protest with a laugh, then he'd nuzzle her neck and she'd turn in his arms, that sexy look in her—

"Raylene said you're staying at your parents' house while you're here."

"Huh?" Nick blinked and the vision vanished. Becca hadn't moved an inch. What the hell was he thinking? He needed to leave. Get outside and get some fresh air. He took a small step back, then another. "Oh, yeah. My parents. For a while. And I'd better get going before someone starts looking for me."

After tapping her wooden spoon on the edge of the pot and putting on a lid, Becca turned around. "I'm in your debt again and can only say thank you. That's not right."

' "Don't worry about it." He shifted his toolbox to the other hand, shocked by his own crazy imagination. One more reason to stay away from her whenever possible. "If you have any questions about Ann-Marie's list, give her a call. She said she'd be happy to help."

Becca nodded.

Nick started for the living room, spied Danny watching TV, and turned back. "Would it be okay if I showed Danny my truck? I think he'd get a kick out of all the tools and stuff in it."

At the mention of her son, she offered a grateful smile. "Of course. Just make sure he puts his coat on."

Nick waited while Danny buttoned up in an almost-too-small coat. As the two of them walked down the porch steps, Nick promised himself that this would be it. He had rescued Becca on a lonely country road, had her flat tire fixed, her oil changed and her car checked over for any other problems. He'd given her a list of places to move and repaired her washing machine. He'd even taken a special liking to her son.

But no more.

Tomorrow he'd be at the job site for the new housing development, getting everything set up for Monday's full day. There wouldn't be time to help Becca. A good thing, too, because every time he did something for her, the past crept closer, and he forgot about the most important part— she had dumped him, and not in a nice way. He couldn't forget about that. Not and get his house.

"ANY LUCK?"

Becca shook her head as she pushed the off button on Raylene's cordless phone and crossed another possibility off the list. Raylene had begged her to come spend the day with her, promising to help in any way she could with the house hunt. Becca knew it was a waste of time. Katyville had become a haven for city people, and property values had soared. She didn't blame them. Katyville was the perfect distance for commuting to Wichita jobs—as her ex-husband had when they were married—or to cultural events. Yet it offered a close-knit community, where crime was almost nil. For those parents concerned with education, Katyville's schools were highly rated, with smaller classes where friendships were formed more easily, many lasting a lifetime. Kids could play outside unattended, without parents worrying about the dangers so often found in the cities. But with the rise in property values, even the smallest and dingiest of houses now sold or rented for way more than she could ever dream of paying—a different world from five years ago. She couldn't have made the payment on the house where she lived with her husband. The sale of it had gone to pay off the mortgage. What was left went to clearing their debt, leaving her very little. She'd been lucky the Watkins place had been so cheap, but only because it was older and outside of Katyville's city limits. And Vera Watkins had known her family and trusted her as a renter, when she wouldn't have trusted a newcomer.

"I can loan you—"

"No," Becca said. "What good will that do? I'll only owe you, too, and I don't have a way to pay you back."

"But the money is in savings. It's not like we need it," Raylene argued.

"It's for your anniversary trip. Your cruise. I'd never forgive myself if you couldn't take it because of me."

Becca knew her only choice was to move to Wichita, and neither she nor Raylene were wild about that idea. They were small-town girls, not city girls, not to mention that they'd see a lot less of each other.

To Becca's relief, Raylene gave up on the loan angle, but it didn't take her long to try another one. "What about the jobs you applied for? Have you heard anything?"

Becca got up from the sofa and paced to the other side of the room. "It's too close to Christmas for anybody to hire now. And with the economy still shaky… It's just one more reason for you to keep your savings," Becca pointed out. "Things can change overnight."

"I know. Jeff has been lucky. So far."

"I'd better start for home," she said, picking up the toys April and Danny had discarded in favor of the movie Raylene had rented for them. "It'll be dark soon, and after the other night, I don't like driving after dark if it isn't necessary."

"You never know. Maybe Nick would rescue you again."

On her hands and knees, Becca looked over at her friend, who had joined her on the floor to hunt for missing blocks. "There's been too much of that already. I don't know how I'll ever repay him for what he's done."

Raylene sat back on her heels and nailed Becca with a look that made her want to squirm. "Did it ever occur to you that he might have done those things because he wanted to?"

Becca couldn't help the unladylike snort that escaped her. "Right. No, it was more like he didn't have a choice. And why would he want to help me? I broke up with him, and I lied to do it."

"I'll bet by now he's figured out what really happened," Raylene replied with a calculating gleam in her eyes.

"Oh, and I'm sure that's made me look completely innocent." Becca shook her head. "No, I was the one who dumped him, just like my father wanted. I just didn't feel I had a choice, not with the way things were with my father." At the time, he had been like a lost soul and hadn't been able to cope with the death of his wife three years before, when Becca was fourteen. "He only wanted what he thought was best for me, when he told me to break it off with Nick. And he was always used to getting his way."

"He never thought Nick would make anything of himself," Raylene said. "But he was wrong."

Becca sighed, thinking of how things had been. "I didn't want Nick to know what my father thought of him. And I'd hoped that, in time, maybe by the end of that summer, I could get my father to see the person Nick really was."

"You never had a chance," Raylene reminded her. "Nick left, took off for college and never came back."

"And it's been pretty clear Nick isn't all that happy to be around me again, even with the help he's given me. With a little luck, he won't be in town much longer."

Raylene was silent for a moment, then slid her a strange look. "You never know."

Becca ignored her. Nick wasn't interested and that was best, considering their past.

With everyone and their belongings in the car except Danny, Becca stood at Raylene's door and thanked her again. She didn't know if she could have survived the past two years without her best friend.

Raylene brushed off her thanks with a wave of her hand. "You'll make it to the final committee meeting on Tuesday night for the Christmas gala, won't you?"

Becca had hoped Raylene had forgotten about it. In the past, Becca had loved being involved in all the community events, but once the whispers of her marriage going bad had begun, she had spent less and less time doing the things she had once enjoyed. She didn't feel comfortable around anyone, except her best friend. She had been taught to keep in mind what others would think of her before saying or doing anything, because in a small town, gossip tended to spread like wildfire. Her failed marriage had been like a lighted match. Living outside of town had offered a little relief. And she was too worried to think about anything else that wasn't about her present predicament, or her future, to spend time planning an event she most likely wouldn't attend.

Shaking her head, she refused to look her friend in the eye. "No, there's just too much to do before we have to—" the words stuck in her throat "—before we have to move."

"All right, considering, but you absolutely have to go to the gala. Everyone is expecting you. You can't just disappear because—"

"I'll try," Becca said, cutting her off and taking Danny's hand. But it was the last thing she wanted to do.

Raylene wasn't going to let her get away with it, though. "I'll pick you up at five on Saturday."

On the drive home, Becca could barely see for the glare from the last rays of the day's winter sun in her eyes. Behind her in the backseat, Danny had fallen asleep, his head resting against the door. Her children hadn't made a sound since they'd left Raylene's, and Becca was glad for the silence, even though it had only been ten minutes' worth. They'd be home in less than another five and, once there, the kids would be awake and begging for supper.

Glancing in the rearview mirror to check on them again, she noticed a vehicle behind them, picking up speed.

"Dumb teenagers," she muttered. Knowing her turn was ahead, she couldn't speed up. She made certain she used her blinker well in advance, hoping the driver behind her would see it. The last thing she needed was some speed-crazy teenager rear-ending her.

Luckily the other vehicle slowed when she did, but when she made the turn, it followed her. The double hedgerow blocked what little was left of the daylight, and she focused on the road ahead. It was the perfect time for deer to emerge seemingly from nowhere, and if she wasn't watching, she could hit one before she saw it. When she heard the horn honking behind her, her grip on the steering wheel tightened. Daring to glance in the mirror again, she nearly slammed on her brakes when she realized it was Nick's truck following her. Butterflies took flight in her stomach and set her heart racing as she slowed her car and pulled to the shoulder of the gravel road.

Nick stopped behind her, and she rolled down her window as he got out of his truck and walked to her car.

"You're hard to catch," Nick said when he reached her door.

"I thought you were some crazy kid."

Nick raked a hand through his hair. "Crazy, yes. Kid, no." Stuffing his hands in the pockets of his jeans, he looked over the top of her car and took a deep breath, which he blew out in a rush. "Here's the deal. I'm in a bind and need your help."

"My help?" she asked, when he looked down at her. "I can't imagine… But I certainly can't say no after everything you've done for me over the past two days." She tried for a smile, but even she couldn't miss the hesitancy in her own voice. "What is it?"

With his mouth set in a grim line, he shook his head. "The woman who's my work-site secretary—you know, she helps keep the records, makes coffee, answers the phone. She was supposed to arrive today, at the very latest. She called this afternoon and told me she has decided she doesn't want to leave Denver. I'm short some of the crew as it is and need someone to screen prospective employees."

Becca wasn't sure what he was getting at. What work site? What crew? "And?" she prompted.

He lowered his head, and she could hear the sound of the gravel on the road being moved around. She smiled, remembering Nick's habit of toeing the ground when he had something he wanted to say but was having a hard time saying it. He had done it when he had asked her out on their first date. He had done it when she had told him she didn't want to see him again. But that time, he hadn't spoken. He had just walked away.

"And, well, I'm desperate," he answered. "And I know you could use the extra money, especially with Christmas so close." He looked up and caught her gaze with his.

"You're offering me a job?" she asked, barely able to speak. "But—but I thought you were just here for a visit."

"Who told you that?"

"Why, nobody. I just thought—" Her mind raced. Oh, heavens! Was he planning to live in Katyville? But what about his— "Is your wife joining you?" It was out of her mouth before she realized and it was too late to take it back.

His mouth turned down in a deep frown and he looked away. "No."

"Oh." As soon as she said it, she knew she sounded like a fool. Where was his wife? she wanted to ask. Why wasn't she joining him? But she kept silent. It didn't make a bit of difference. "What about your company in Denver?"

"I moved it here to Katyville. I wanted to be closer to my family, and there's a need for construction companies here." He looked at her again. "So what about the job? Do you want it?"

"I don't know anything about construction."

"You'll learn."

Even with her heart thudding at the chance to change her situation, Becca still had reservations. "I'll have to find a babysitter," she reminded him.

"Gabby said she'd be happy to do it."

She hated to accept anything else from him or his family. "Your sister has enough on her hands with her own family."

"'The more, the merrier,' Gabby always says."

Becca knew she couldn't turn down a job offer, not in her situation. But she wasn't sure she would be able to survive seeing Nick on a regular basis. And considering the not-so-happy look on his face, she wasn't sure he would survive, either, but for very different reasons.

Taking a deep breath, she made her decision. "Okay. I'll take it."

Chapter Four

While Nick showed Becca around the office, he wondered for the hundredth time just how crazy he must have been to offer Becca the job. But desperation led men to do desperate things, and when Carol, his former secretary, had called to say she wouldn't be leaving Denver, Becca and her situation—a situation he had become a part of—had somehow popped into his mind.

Still managing to keep a safe distance from her in the tiny confines of the job-site trailer, he finished telling her about her duties. She was sharp but he knew there would be moments when the pace would pick up. He would try to keep as much of that from happening as he could, just as he had with Carol. Becca had enough to handle as it was, and he didn't want to add to it. Now that she had a job, he hoped it would be easier for her to find a new place to live. Once she was out from under all the pressure of finding a place and moving to it, he would tell her the truth. After all, it would only be a few weeks. Until then, he would bide his time and hope nobody beat him to it. Only Tony and Mrs. Watkins knew about the house, so there wasn't anything to worry about.

"So it's really just answering the phone, filing, doing some preinterviews with the applicants and making a few notes on that to pass on to me," he explained, ready to leave her to do her job.

"And keeping a fresh pot of hot coffee," she added with a nervous smile.

"And that." He couldn't help his own smile. She caught on quick. "If things get too hectic, and you start having second thoughts about this, just lock the door until everything settles down. It's your office. You're in charge. Although I do expect a fair day's work for a fair day's pay."

Her expression serious, she nodded. "I'll do my best."

He hoped her best would be good enough. From what she had told him, she didn't have any job experience. On the other hand, he knew she was smart and the job didn't require any special education. He was almost convinced she would do fine. He just wasn't sure about how *he'd* do.

"I—I do have a question." Her hesitancy was clear, not only in her voice, but in her eyes.

"Ask away."

She smiled that shy smile that he knew so well. "How many employees are there?"

"Anywhere between ten and thirty, depending on what stage we're on. Right now, we're at about fifteen or so. I lose track. But we'll be adding more."

"They all came with you from Denver?"

He liked that she was interested. "Some, but I'm hoping to employ mostly locals. That was one of the reasons I decided to bring the company here. Employment."

She nodded and seemed to look pleased. For some

reason that pleased him, but he didn't examine it. "One more thing, before I leave you alone to settle in."

"What's that?" she asked, caution in her eyes.

He wasn't quite sure how to say it, but it needed to be said. "Your clothes," he said, after a short hesitation.

She looked down at the pretty blue suit she was wearing and tugged at the bottom of the jacket. "What's wrong with it? It isn't new, but—"

"It's not that." Seeing her eyes widen when she looked up at him, he realized she was getting the wrong idea. There was no telling what she thought he was going to say. If it wasn't for the fact that a part of him wanted to hang out in the office with her for the rest of the day, while the rest of him knew that was a bad idea and that he needed to get out on the site, he might have laughed. But it wasn't funny. He was finding that he was constantly having to remind himself that this was a business arrangement, not a chance to spend time with her. He wanted not to like her, but that was proving to be impossible.

"Around here, we're about as casual as we can get," he explained. Without meaning to, his gaze traveled to the bottom of her skirt and her long legs, then he jerked his attention back up to her face, feeling a little ashamed for being tempted. "I'm guessing you'd get cold in a skirt."

Even he heard the edge in his voice, and he coughed to cover it. A quick blush rose to color her cheeks, and she ducked her head. There was no doubt now that he'd been crazy to offer her the job. And he was making a mess of what he was trying to tell her.

"What I mean is," he hurried to say, "well, jeans and sweatshirts are fine. This trailer is heated, but there'll be times when the crew will be in and out of here, and the cold wind will blow right in with them. It gets dirty around here, too, especially when the wind is blowing."

"I'll remember that." She walked around the desk to the chair and stood looking at him. "Anything else I should know?"

At first he thought she was dismissing him, but he detected a waver in her voice and realized that she was even more nervous than he was. "Not that I can think of. Sorry I can't help more right now, but if you need anything—" He followed her around the desk to stand next to her, careful that he didn't get too close. Pulling out a drawer, he reached in and took out a small two-way radio and placed it on the desk. "I have the match to it here," he said, patting his shirt pocket. "If you need anything, just give me a shout. There's the talk button."

"Thanks."

He thought he heard some relief in the word, but he couldn't be sure. Knowing it was time to leave and let her get used to the place, he still hesitated.

And then sanity suddenly returned, and he forced his feet to move. If this was the way it was going to be, maybe this would only be a temporary job for her. At that moment, it sounded good to him.

But it sounded bad, too.

With his hand on the doorknob, he turned back to look at her. She had seated herself at the desk with her elbows propped on the top of it, her chin resting on her folded hands, looking like the girl he remembered from ten years before. He needed to get out. Now.

"Give me a shout if you need anything," he said a second

time. He grabbed his hard hat, which was hanging by the door, and hurried outside, taking the two metal steps in one leap.

"Problems?" his crew foreman asked as he approached.

Nick shook his head, determined to put Becca out of his mind. "Let's get this job rolling."

As he and Clint did their morning rounds of the site, he suddenly had one bright thought among all the others in his head. If his mother should discover that he was the landlord who was turning Becca out, at least he could always say that he was doing all he could to help.

Too busy with lining out the job site and hunting down missing supplies, Nick didn't touch base with Becca again until the end of the day.

He wasn't prepared for the sight that presented itself when he walked into the job trailer. Becca, bent over the lower drawer of the file cabinet, offered a view that Nick hadn't anticipated.

He couldn't stop staring.

Memories of the girl he had spent summer evenings with, parked in his old, beat-up sedan on Morgan Creek Road, scrolled through his mind. He could almost hear the wind whispering through the nearby trees mingling with the soft sounds of a passion they had never quenched, never moving beyond smoldering kisses and needy touches.

"Coffee?"

He shook his head, clearing it of the past, and noticed that Becca had turned around to face him.

"Are you all right?" she asked, stepping closer to peer at him.

"Coffee. Yes," he croaked. And he wondered if he was going to survive working with her.

For a moment, she hesitated, her concern evident. After a shrug, she turned and walked across the room to the coffeemaker. He watched every movement her body made, traces of those memories refusing to leave.

"Sounds like you're catching a cold," she said over her shoulder as she poured him a cup of coffee.

"I'm okay," he managed to say. As soon as she turned around with the mug in hand, he made sure he wasn't looking directly at her. Fearing she might read something in his face, he took the coffee from her and moved away.

"I was just, um, trying to familiarize myself with the filing system," she said from behind him.

Did she think he thought she was snooping? There was nothing in his company files that anybody couldn't see. Even the employee files were straightforward and hid no secrets. Besides, Becca had never struck him as someone who would stoop to something like that. She had always been honest with him. To a fault. When she had tired of him, years ago, she had come right out and told him so.

"The office looks great," he said, making sure the conversation stayed on business. "I see you found somewhere to put all the stuff from the boxes. Wherever you can find a place is okay. You'll be the one using it, so whatever works best for you."

"I'll finish up tomorrow," she said, taking a seat behind the desk.

He cleared his throat again and she looked up at him. "Any calls?" he asked, unable to make eye contact with her.

She slid two pieces of paper across the desk toward him. "These two. Prospective employees. I told them to come in and fill out applications."

He nodded. Even though she didn't have any experience, she seemed to be able to handle things well. There was no telling how long she'd continue to work for him. Once she learned the truth, he suspected she would leave, but until then, he was pleased with her competence. If he could just get past this crazy attraction to her, things might work out for both of them.

When she glanced up at the clock on the wall, he looked, too, and realized it was quitting time. Relief swept through him. *Made it through the first day.*

He stepped aside while she pulled her purse from one of the desk drawers and fetched her coat. "Same time tomorrow?" he asked as she started for the door.

"I'll be here," she answered, her voice sounding tired but determined.

Knowing she had a family to take care of when she got home, he almost felt bad. But he reminded himself that, with a job, she would be able to find a new place to live. And that was his goal, wasn't it?

When she'd gone, he sat behind the desk she had vacated and looked around the job trailer. It really did look great. Even better than when Carol had worked for him. All he could do was hope that everything continued to go well—for both of them.

NICK STOOD TO CARRY his empty plate and silverware from the dinner table to the kitchen. It was a habit that had been formed when he was young. In his mother's house, with six kids, everyone picked up after themselves.

"I heard you hired a new secretary," his mother said, stopping him in his tracks before he could take a step.

Who had told her that? He hadn't mentioned it to anyone except Tony. Not that he had been trying to keep it a secret.

"Uh, yeah," he answered, unable to look at her, afraid she might see something in his face that would give him away. The woman could see guilt with her eyes closed. And he was definitely guilty. Or at least he would be in his mother's eyes if she knew everything.

"So tell me," she urged.

Steeling himself for what might become a lecture, he took a deep breath and shrugged, looking right into her eyes as he eased himself away from the table and toward the kitchen. "Tell you what, Mama? I hired a new secretary. No big deal. Carol called from Denver to say she decided she couldn't move, so I needed someone else."

Relieved to have made it to the kitchen and away from his mother's scrutiny, he put his dishes in the sink. He would just head up to his room and do some reading. Or maybe watch a little television.

But just as he was starting up the back stairs, his mother's voice stopped him again.

"Nicky, you're going to bed? It's early yet. Come in and talk to your papa and me. Tell us about this new secretary."

That was the last thing he wanted to do. "I was just going to read for a while, Mama. I'll be down later."

"You're avoiding us?"

Once again, he faced her. "Of course not."

"Then come into the living room." She gestured for him to follow her. "Gabby and Joseph are coming by with the *bambini*," she said over her shoulder.

At the mention of Gabby's name, he knew where his mother had gotten her information. His sister was watching

Becca's kids. Just how much had his sister told their mother? There was only one way to find out.

With a silent groan, he followed his mother into the living room. As he settled onto the sofa, he heard his sister and her family come in the front door.

"Come in, come in," his mother said, waving them into the room. "Nicky was just getting ready to tell us about his new secretary."

"How did Becca do?" Gabby asked, putting her daughter on the sofa beside him, while she took off her coat and fussed with the baby boy her husband handed her. "She looked tired when she came by to pick up her kids."

"Becca?" his mother said, looking from daughter to son. "Becca Tyler? Is that who you hired, Nicky?"

Helping his two-year-old niece, Catarina, out of her coat while Gabby's husband helped with the baby, Nick decided the best thing was to be honest. As honest as he could be, anyway. "Yes, Becca Tyler."

His mother nodded. "I'm glad to hear that, Nicky. She's had a hard time. That husband of hers was…*difettoso.*"

Nick had to laugh. "Defective, huh?"

Gabby settled on the other side of her daughter. "She's well rid of him. And I'm so glad you offered her a job. You won't be disappointed."

He turned to look at her, surprised that his sister knew Becca any more than simply her name. "You know her that well?"

Nodding, Gabby smiled. "Do you think I'd offer to take care of just anybody's children? She used to be involved in so many things in Katyville. Very quiet, very sweet. She could talk anybody into almost anything with only a smile."

His mother leaned forward, her face now serious. "She helped with the turkey shoot every year, and she doesn't even belong to the parish." Leaning back, she gave Nick a smile that made him want to run and hide. "It's nice that you're getting to know her again, Nicky."

He knew that look. His mother enjoyed bringing two people together. And he wasn't having any of it. "I needed a secretary, Mama. That's all. And she needed a job."

She nodded, her knowing smile remaining, and leaned back in her chair. "You knew her well."

"That was a long time ago," he insisted, "so stop trying to make something of it. Please."

His mother turned to Gabby, obviously ignoring him. "I was so worried when she moved out of town and into that big old house. It would be falling apart, after all the years of not being lived in."

"The house is fine," Nick said, without thinking. When his mother turned back to look at him, he knew he had to explain himself. "I found her a few miles from town last Friday night with a flat tire and no spare, so I drove her into town. Tony fixed her tire and I took her car to her."

Nick's father shifted uneasily in his chair. "Are you talking about Becca Malone?"

Nick's mother stood and went to plump the pillow behind his back. An injury before he passed the garage on to Tony had left him with more stiffness than he would acknowledge to his family. "Yes, Carmine," his wife told him, kissing the top of his head before moving away. "You remember her, don't you?"

He nodded. "Nico was sweet on her."

Nick ducked his head so no one would see his embarrassment. There was one thing that would always be true about his family. They knew way more about things than they should, which they never forgot and never thought twice about bringing up, to the embarrassment of others.

"Her father moved to…" Nick's father turned to his wife, who had perched on the arm of his chair. "Where was that again, *cara?*"

"Australia," she answered. "Not long after her first little one arrived. I hear he married a woman there a few years ago."

His sigh was deep. "Some men can do that." He looked at his wife of more than thirty years. "Something I could never do."

She placed one hand in his and patted his cheek lovingly with the other. "I pray you never have to worry about that."

"I always worry."

"You shouldn't."

Nick was reminded of the story his father had told about the first time he met Elena Vescovi. It was hard to believe that this woman—strong and loving with the flashing dark eyes—was the same quiet, shy girl Carmine Morelli had fallen in love with at first sight.

Nick's mother raised her head to look at him. "She had to move after her husband ran off and left her. I heard he also left many bills to be paid, and she had to sell their house to pay them. It was such a pretty house, too."

Gabby slipped her arm around her daughter. "The longer she was married, the more unhappy she seemed to be. But she never said a word and always had a smile and kind words for everyone. Even him."

His mother shook her head and sighed. "She never should have married that…*uomo.* He was no good."

Nick did his best to hide a smile. It wasn't the word his mother used, which meant *man,* but it was the way in which she said it. There was no doubt how she felt about Becca's ex-husband, and even Nick had to admit that he agreed, even though he had never met him.

"She's doing okay then?" his mother asked, looking from him to Gabby.

"As well as can be expected, I think," Gabby answered. She leaned forward and shot him a grin, before leaning back. "As long as Nick, the slave driver, doesn't work her to death."

He opened his mouth to defend himself, but Gabby's daughter saved him. "*Nonna,* have to *potty!*"

After giving her husband a hug, Nick's mother held her hand out to her little granddaughter. "Then come with me." Turning to Nick before they left the room, she gave him a stern look. "You be nice to her, Nicky."

He knew she meant Becca. "Of course, Mama."

When the two were out of the room, Joseph chuckled. "She matchmaking again, Nick?"

"Always," Nick answered, shaking his head. His mother's high esteem of Becca only made things worse. What if she should learn that he had purchased the Watkins house and was forcing Becca to leave?

Heaven help him.

Maybe he could do something. Something to help Becca even more. Then, if his mother did discover what he'd done, he would have one more thing that would help him get back in her good graces. And being in Mama's good graces was a must in the Morelli family.

Now that he had spent time with Becca, the pain she had wrought when they were young was beginning to ease. Still, he wouldn't get caught up and let his attraction to her bring about a repeat of the past. He could *like* her. There wasn't anything wrong with that. He could help her. It sure seemed she needed it more than he'd imagined. As long as he didn't fall for her again.

And he knew exactly what to do.

BECCA HAD VOWED to become accustomed to being around Nick again. He had given her a job—something she desperately needed—and she wouldn't give him any reason to fire her. She would just have to get used to being cramped in the tiny trailer with him, afraid of doing or saying the wrong thing that might give away that she had never completely gotten over him, even though she had thought she had. She couldn't ever let him know that.

"He should be here any minute, Mr. Greshky," she said, handing the prospective employee a cup of coffee.

"Thank you," he said, taking it from her.

She smiled at him, hoping to make him feel more at ease as he sat stiffly in the chair across the desk from her. He had been waiting at the door to the trailer when she arrived. It had been clear from his nervousness that he needed a job, even before he had asked to fill out an application. She understood that and hoped Nick would be able to find a place for him on the crew.

She had already had him fill out the paperwork, had read it and thought he had some qualifications. But what did she know? Only Nick could make that decision.

When the door opened and Nick walked in, the room seemed to shrink around her. Shaking off the feeling, she stood and went to the coffeemaker to pour him a cup. Handing it to him, she nodded toward the man seated in the chair. "Mr. Greshky has filled out an application and would like to speak with you," she explained, and gave Nick the application.

Nick looked at the man, and then at her. "I really need to be getting outside." Turning to the man, he said, "I'm running a little behind this morning."

Becca could see how disappointed the man was, but he stood and straightened his shoulders. "I understand. Maybe when you have the time."

Becca took a chance and gave Nick a pleading look. She sensed the man needed a job, possibly as badly as she had.

Again, Nick looked from her to the man. "Well, I guess I have a few minutes. Come on into my office," he told the man. "Bring your coffee and let's see what I can do for you."

Becca mouthed a "thank you" to Nick as he passed, and the man followed him down the narrow hallway to Nick's private office. While they were gone, she wished she could hear their conversation, but she couldn't, so she busied herself with familiarizing herself with the names of the other employees. Still, she felt anxious for the man and hoped that Nick could help.

When the two men appeared some time later, Becca didn't miss the smile on the man's face. After he had thanked her and Nick both, and shook Nick's hand, she couldn't help but feel happy. "He was qualified, then?" she asked Nick when the man had gone.

"Enough," Nick said. "But I could tell he needed the job,

and I always try to employ those who do. Sometimes they make the best workers."

Becca hoped she would be among them. She wanted to be a good employee. Wanted it desperately. And she wanted to be able to do her job as professionally as possible, although she had never worked in an office before.

"Is there anything I should know about today?" Nick asked.

"There's a note here on the calendar about an appointment with a prospective employee."

"Yeah. Right. I forgot about that. Glad you caught it. He'll be here about ten."

"Eleven," she corrected.

Nick nodded, but he seemed preoccupied. "I'll lose track of time, so just give me a shout on the two-way when he gets here."

The door opened behind him and he turned as his foreman walked in. Slipping off his hard hat, the man nodded to Becca. "Mornin', ma'am."

"Good morning, Clint," she answered with a smile.

Nick turned to look at her, and she thought she detected a frown. But she wasn't sure, because he turned back to Clint immediately.

"...delivering that drywall this afternoon," the foreman was saying. "What are we supposed to do with it?"

Nick definitely frowned at the news. "Why the hell—" He slid an apologetic glance at Becca. "Why are they delivering it now? We won't need it for a good month or more."

The foreman shrugged. "Don't know, boss. Maybe they got their wires crossed. And maybe we're a little behind schedule on this project."

Nick turned to Becca. "Call Evans Drywall. Number's on a card in the…"

"Roledex?" she said, reaching for it.

He nodded. "Yeah. Tell them to hold off on the delivery, until they hear from us. And tell them we *do* want it, but the timing is bad. I'll give Jack Evans a call later to explain."

Becca was reaching for the phone when Clint cleared his throat. "I'll wait outside."

"No, hang on," Nick said, pulling his gloves from his pocket and grabbing his hard hat. "If they give you any trouble, Becca, let me know." Without waiting for a reply from her, he motioned for Clint to open the door. "Guess we'd better see what else will go wrong today."

After they were gone, Becca made the call and assured Mr. Evans that the supplies would be needed, then reached for the mail and sorted it. Nick had explained the day before that he had a bookkeeper who figured the pay and cut the paychecks, but Becca would need to total up the hours for each employee on a spreadsheet. Turning on the computer at the corner of her desk, she found the correct file and lost herself in her work.

It was nearly eleven when she finished, so she picked up the two-way and reminded Nick of his upcoming appointment. She wondered if this prospective employee would do as well as the one earlier and just how many more Nick was planning to hire. The rumors that Nick had had a successful business in Colorado had obviously been true. After seeing how he had made time for Martin Greshky earlier, she understood why. He cared about the people who worked for him.

Nick came in the door and didn't bother to look at her before heading down the hall. "Would you bring me some coffee, Becca?"

Before she had it poured, his appointment arrived. Her first impression of this man wasn't good. He had a smug look on his face that made her dislike him instantly, but she greeted him politely and instructed him to take a seat. When she asked him if he would like some coffee, he said he would, so she went to pour him a cup.

"You're definitely an improvement over the old secretary," he told her.

Becca glanced behind her, noticing that he was still standing, and she tried to smile. Feeling uneasy, she quickly turned to hand him the hot cup. He took it from her and followed her as she hurried down the hall with Nick's coffee and to let him know his appointment had arrived. She could feel the man behind her looking at her, and it made her uncomfortable.

Nick looked up with a frown when she opened his office door, but he was looking past her, not at her. "Come on in, Luke."

As Becca closed the door, leaving the men to talk, she could hear them.

"Gotcha a pretty one, hey?"

There was a short silence before Nick answered. "Are you here for a job or to hit on my secretary?"

The man laughed, and Becca winced at the sound. "Why, a job, of course, but it never hurts to look," he said.

She hurried away from the door, missing Nick's response. If he knew the man, she suspected he would hire him, especially if he was a former employee. And just because she didn't like him, it didn't mean that he wasn't a good worker. Wasn't that what Nick wanted?

Ten minutes later, the two men emerged from Nick's

office. As the man was walking out the door, he turned to wink at her. "I'll be seeing you."

When he was gone, Nick turned to Becca with a sigh. "He won't last long."

"You do know him, then." She was curious, but she wouldn't ask.

"He used to work on one of my crews in Colorado. Fortunately, he isn't real reliable."

Fortunately? She wasn't sure she understood. "I know it isn't my place to ask, but if he isn't reliable, why did you hire him again today?"

Nick seemed to be preoccupied as he buttoned his coat and pulled on his gloves. "He came all the way from Boulder, looking for work. He needed a job. I couldn't send him off without at least giving him a try again. Maybe he's changed."

Becca wanted to say she doubted it, from what she'd seen of the man, but she remained silent. Could Nick be feeling the same way about her?

He had moved to the door and stopped. "I'll be out most of the day," he told her as he grabbed his hard hat and reached for the knob. "Did you get in touch with Evans Drywall?"

Becca nodded, forcing her mind back on the business at hand, instead of worrying about herself and the reason Nick had hired her. "They said they'd hold it for you, until either you needed it or had someplace to store it."

"Good." His brow furrowed in thought. "Unless there's an emergency, I won't be back in the office. If you need something—"

"I'll give you a shout on the two-way," she finished for him.

She was surprised to see him smile. He had seemed to be doing more frowning than usual.

"Just make sure you go home on time."

He was out the door before she could answer, and she let out her breath, unaware that she had been holding it. Nick was a good employer, who cared about his employees. There was no question about that. And, as he had with Martin Greshky, he had given her a job when she needed one, even though she didn't have the qualifications. All she could do was her best. But if that wasn't enough, how long would Nick continue to keep her?

The door flew open and Nick poked his head inside. "You're doing a good job, Becca."

The door closed as quickly as it had opened, and he was gone. She sat at her desk, staring at it. Then a slow smile settled on her lips.

Chapter Five

Three-year-old April clung to Becca's leg. "Don't go, Mommeeeee!"

Becca's heart broke at her daughter's tears, and she glanced at Gabby, who watched with a look of commiseration on her face. "Did something happen yesterday?" Becca asked.

Shaking her head, Gabby knelt down to talk to April. "Don't you want to stay and play with Cat?"

April shook her head, her ponytail swinging, and clung tighter to Becca. Tears streamed down her face as she looked up at her mom. "Cat is my best friend."

Becca would have laughed at the duplicity, but her daughter's tears didn't allow it, and she leaned down as best she could with April clamped to her knees. "Yes, sweetie, I know she is. That's why you like to stay here. But I can't stay. I have to go to work. And you know I'll be back later, after your nap, and then we'll go home and have supper."

Gabby put her hand on the girl's forehead and looked at Becca. "She is a little warm."

Becca felt like crying herself. It was only her fourth day on the job. What would Nick think when she told him she couldn't be there? "She's caught Daisy's cold," she said as she began to gather up her children's belongings.

Gabby laid her hand on Becca's arm. "What are you doing?"

Battling the tears that threatened, Becca shook her head. "You don't want a sick child here. Yours will only catch it and—"

"And what? They'll catch a cold. If not from April, then from someone else." Gabby put her arm around April and spoke to her in a gentle tone of voice. "Cat will cry if you leave, and you don't want her to be sad, do you?"

April sniffed and shook her head.

"And we have chocolate pudding today," Gabby continued. "You can't miss that!" She looked up at Becca. "I have some cold medicine I can give her. It'll make her feel better. And Mama always gave us something when we first started to get sick. It's an old family thing, but our colds were usually gone in a couple of days. If that's okay with you."

Becca nodded, grateful to Gabby for being so understanding. As Gabby gently drew April away, Becca stepped out of her daughter's grasp.

"She'll be fine," Gabby said, scooping the girl into her arms. "I'll call you if she isn't, okay?"

"Thank you," Becca whispered as she opened the door. "I hate leaving them—" It took everything she had to keep from bursting in to tears.

"I know you do."

Once outside the door, Becca drew herself up, determined not to worry. She knew her kids were in good hands. Gabby was a good person, just as her brother was. The entire Morelli family always had been. There were a few who said the Morellis lived on the wrong side of the tracks, but Becca had always envied their big family and the love they shared. She'd also known there would be mornings like this. Having spent so much time with her children, they weren't accustomed to her being gone all day. But there wasn't anything she could do about that, and she expected they would adjust in time.

Once at work, Becca remained busy. Several job applications were left on her desk, and the mail brought even more. During one of Nick's sporadic and brief visits to the job trailer, she pointed them out to him.

Running a hand through his thick, dark hair, he sighed. "I've got my hands full out on the site. We had three unscheduled deliveries early this morning, and we're trying to find someplace big enough to hold all the supplies."

"Is there anything I can do to help?"

"No." He turned toward the hall, and then stopped. "Yes. Once we get this mess figured out, I'll need more men. Make a list of the applicants. I don't have time to do interviews, but I'll have to. Spread the appointments out over tomorrow and early next week, if you can. Afternoons will be best. I hope."

She began gathering the applications on her desk. "Maybe right after lunch?"

"Yeah, that would be the best time. No more than a couple of hours a day. That's all I can spare right now. Figure fifteen minutes or so for each. I don't have time to make them any longer."

"That would be eight a day, so two days might cover it."

He looked at her, a slow, sexy smile replacing his frown. "You're quick."

It wasn't what he'd said that had her speechless and unable to answer. It was the look in his eyes that held hers.

"I'll—I'll get right on it," she finally managed to say.

He broke the gaze and released her. "Good. Oh, and bring me a cup of coffee?"

Becca smiled in relief. "Right away."

Once he was safely in his office with his steaming coffee mug, Becca got down to work, setting up a schedule, going through the applications and calling to make the appointments. Engrossed in her work, she didn't realize that lunchtime had come and gone. It was after one when she took her sandwich from the small refrigerator in the corner.

Before she could sit down at her desk to eat her lunch as she worked, the door opened.

"How's it going?" Raylene asked, waltzing in and settling on the chair across from Becca's desk, a wide grin on her face.

Becca was surprised to see her. "What are you doing here?"

Raylene shrugged off her coat and reached for her purse. "I was out running errands and stopped off at your place to pick up your mail. You said on the phone last night that you were so tired, you'd forgotten to get it out of the box for two days, so here."

Becca took the pile of envelopes and advertising from her and set it aside. "I'll look it over later. I've been busy this morning."

"Nick's a real tough boss, huh?"

Laughing, Becca shook her head. "Not hardly. He's a good boss."

"Yeah? How good?"

Becca recognized the wicked glint in Raylene's eyes. "Don't even think it," she warned.

"You're no fun, you know that?"

Becca couldn't keep from laughing. "You can stop pouting. Just be happy that with a little luck, I'll find someplace to move soon."

"That's good." Raylene looked around the small office. "So where is this great boss of yours? And how do you survive working in such close quarters?"

Becca shushed her with a finger to her lips and looked over her shoulder to see if Nick might have left his private office. As far as she knew, he'd missed lunch, and she expected him to appear at any moment. "He's in his office down the hall," she answered, her voice almost a whisper. "As for the other, it isn't easy."

"Ha! I knew it!"

Standing, Becca walked around the desk and pulled Raylene to her feet. "We'll discuss it another time. I need to get back to work."

Raylene gathered her things and allowed Becca to steer her toward the door. "It's tough with an ogre of a boss, huh?"

"Hush!"

"Okay, call me when you get home tonight." Raylene slipped on her coat and grabbed the doorknob. "And don't forget."

When her best friend had gone, Becca settled at her desk again, flipping through the mail Raylene had brought. Mixed with the junk mail and overdue bills was one with a return address she recognized. One look at it and her heart dropped.

She stood, her knees shaking along with her hands.

What could her new landlord's attorney want now? What bad news would she find when she opened the envelope and pulled out the paper inside? "I'm trying," she whispered.

Her heart thudded as she slipped out the letter printed on expensive vellum, and the words blurred before her eyes. Finally forcing herself to focus, she began reading it.

"Who was that?"

She jerked her head up at the sound of the familiar male voice and discovered Nick watching her. Speechless at what she read and not thinking clearly, she launched herself into his arms.

Nick caught her, wrapping his arms around her, her feet dangling above the floor, just as her heart was floating. Her happiness was boundless. Too excited to know what she was doing, she kissed him, then laughed with joy. "I've been given an extension on the date to vacate," she said, breathless.

So caught up in her happiness, she wasn't fully aware of Nick lowering his head to capture her lips with his. She gave herself up to the kiss and participated fully, wrapping her arms around his neck and opening her lips to welcome him.

Until she realized what she was doing.

She froze and pushed at his shoulders. He lowered her feet to the floor and loosened his hold on her.

"I—I don't know what— I mean—" She didn't realize she was backing away until she was stopped by her desk. Closing her eyes and wishing she could turn back time, she tried to apologize and explain. "I—I'm so sorry, Nick. I wasn't thinking. I just—"

But Nick was gone.

She took two wobbly steps and sank onto the nearest chair. Could she have done anything worse?

NICK KNEW HE WAS BEING unreasonably hard on his crew, but he couldn't stop. The kiss he had shared with Becca had left him reeling. Even more, the shock on her face when she realized what had happened was burned into his memory. She'd *apologized!* For kissing him back! He'd been the one to overstep the bounds, and *she* was the one who apologized to *him.* Could the situation between them get any worse?

It reminded him too much of the day she had come to him, ten years before, and told him she wasn't interested in seeing him anymore. She had dumped him, in no uncertain terms. He had been crazy in love with her and didn't think he would ever feel pain like he had at the moment. He'd never spoken to her again, avoided her until he left for college, and forbid his family or friends to speak of her. Months later, when the memory dared to play itself in his mind, he remembered how her eyes had glistened, as if she were about to cry. He had immediately and silently declared the memory a fraud and vowed never to think of her again. And he pretty much hadn't, until he'd found her on the road with a flat tire almost a week ago.

His foreman joined him as he stood staring at the job site, thinking about Becca and not the business, as he should have been. "You're mighty grumpy this afternoon. More early deliveries?"

"Sorry," was all Nick could say.

"Anything I can do to help?"

Nick almost laughed. If only Clint could help him, but there was nothing anybody could do. He'd managed to get himself into something he couldn't get out of, and there was nothing to do about it except keep going. He would be a fool to fall for her again, but every day that seemed to be more of a possibility.

He wasn't looking forward to being in the job trailer with her, but he didn't have a choice. And he sure couldn't fire her for something that he had done. Even if he could, he might not be able to find someone to take her place. And he couldn't cause her any more harm just because he wanted her house.

Forcing his mind off his problems with Becca—problems that he'd caused and was now making even worse—he turned to Clint. "I'll be tied up in the office a few hours after lunch for the rest of the week, interviewing applicants."

"We can sure use more help," Clint agreed.

"How's the new guy doing? Greshky?"

"Good. He takes orders without question and gets it done. Better than some, that's for sure."

And if it hadn't been for Becca, Nick knew he might not have hired the man. She might not know it, but she was more of an asset than he had thought she would be. As an employee, anyway. As a woman—

"What about Luke?" he asked, forcing himself to think about the company, instead of the woman that he couldn't get out of his mind.

"He showed up. Did his job."

"For now."

"Yeah. That's Luke. I hope you find better men to hire than him." Clint was silent for a moment. "If you need me to stay late tonight, I can," he offered.

Nick shook his head. "No. In fact, I'm heading home now." He glanced toward the job trailer and saw Becca getting into her car. "It's quitting time, and I didn't even have any lunch."

"See you tomorrow, then," Clint said, and walked off to signal the end of the day to the crew.

By the time Nick reached home, he felt like someone had run over him with a steamroller. It was a relief to sit down to supper and forget about the events of the day while talking with his family. It was only his father and mother at the table, and he enjoyed it that way, especially after the day he'd had. With six kids in the family growing up, mealtimes had never been quiet. Fun, yes. Crazy, you bet. Quiet, no.

"Nicky, I wanted to ask you something," his mother said, passing around the half-empty platter of linguini.

"What's that, Mama?" He took it from her and added a second helping of one of his favorite dishes.

"Could you give me Becca's mailing address?"

His loaded spoon stopped halfway to his plate, and he looked at her. "Why?"

She shrugged and smiled. "To send a Christmas card?"

Dumping the linguini on his plate, he frowned. He knew his mother too well to believe the line she was feeding him. "No, Mama. Tell me why."

"Now, Nicky…"

He looked to his father. "Pop, she's your wife. Tell her to stop playing games."

"She's your mama, Nico. You tell her."

It was obvious his father wasn't willing to help. Sitting back in his chair, Nick crossed him arms on his chest. "Mama…"

"Okay, okay," she relented. "I wanted to send her an invitation to Tony's birthday party the week before Christmas. You object to that?"

"Hell, yes, I object to that."

"Nico, your language," his father reminded him. "You owe your mama respect."

Nick nodded. He'd been out of bounds. But his mother was, too, just thinking of inviting Becca to a family party. "She's an employee, Mama, not part of the family."

"She's a family friend," she retorted. "Tony doesn't mind, and it's *his* birthday party."

Of course Tony didn't mind. He knew the fix Nick was in. Typical baby brother.

Nick decided it was best to be calm about this latest in his mother's matchmaking ventures. Logic would work best. "Becca Malone has never been a family friend, and you know it, Mama," he reminded her. "Sure, she's nice and all that, but a family friend? Never."

She looked at him, cocking her head to one side. He knew that look, and he squirmed beneath it. "Why 'never'?" she asked. "And how do you know? You've been gone for most of the past ten years. There was a time when she might have been a family friend. Maybe even a family member."

He thought of the past, of the day she had dumped him after they'd dated for almost six months, of how he had hoped, planned, dreamed, even loved…for nothing. "Things happen. People change."

"You really don't know her, Nicky. You don't know how things have been since you left."

And he didn't want to. He knew enough. Wasn't that— and what his mother would think of him—the reason he was doing everything he could to help her? "I don't need to know any more than I already do," he said, remaining firm.

"But—"

"Please, Mama. You know it's not good to mix business

and friends. Just ask Pop." He knew it was weak, but it was all he had.

She looked at her husband, who nodded at her, then back at Nick. "Can we have her for dinner sometime?"

"Have who for dinner?"

Nick turned to see Tony walk into the dining room. His brother kissed their mother on the cheek and patted their father on the shoulder. "So what's up? Who are you having for dinner?"

His mother pouted. "Nobody, if Nicky has his way."

Tony looked at Nick, his eyebrows raised in question. Nick shook his head, not wanting to discuss it any longer.

"Is this about—" Tony began. But Nick gave him a warning look and Tony didn't finish.

Nick cleared his throat. "I was just explaining to Mama that it isn't wise to mix business with family."

Tony must have understood, because he nodded in agreement. "But since it is my birthday party..."

"See?" she said to her eldest son. "Tony is in favor of having this guest. You are the only one, Nicky, who doesn't want her here. Why is that?"

Nick knew when he was outnumbered. Pushing his chair back, he tossed his napkin on the table and stood. "Fine. Whatever the rest of you decide to do is okay with me. But don't be surprised if I don't show up for this party."

"Sit down, Nico."

When Nick heard his father, he did as he was told. "I'm sorry, Pop." No one said anything, much to Nick's embarrassment. Carmine Morelli rarely got after his grown children.

Tony broke the silence. "Maybe we should just table this discussion until another time."

"We should," his mother agreed. "Sit down, Tony. How is Beth? Still some morning sickness?"

"Not much," he said, taking a seat across the table from Nick. "She said something about stopping by to see you tomorrow."

"Good. I look forward to it. She's a sweet girl." She slid a look at Nick. "Much like another I know."

Nick had lost his appetite several minutes ago, but his mother's determination nearly caused him to get up and leave. Instead, he chose to ignore her comment.

"You pay her well?"

When no one said anything, Nick looked up to see his mother studying him. "What?"

"Becca. Do you pay her well? Because if anybody needs it, she does."

"Yes, of course I do."

"Maybe you should pay her more."

"More?" Nick had to force himself to keep from raising his voice. If only his mother knew how much he had done for Becca. Then again, it would mean she would find out how embroiled he was in the whole house thing.

"Yes, Nicky. More. Isn't she worth it? I mean, she's a good secretary for you, isn't she?"

He couldn't deny she wasn't. In fact, she surpassed Carol by keeping one step ahead of him.

And she made great coffee.

Taking a deep breath, he prayed he could keep his voice steady. "She hasn't worked for me that long. I'm not a bank, Mama. And I've never heard an employee complain about pay. Not one. I pay all my people well."

Tony's voice was tentative when he spoke. "Really, Mama, Nick's business is his…well, it's his business, that's all."

Tony's comment earned a glare from his mother. Then she sniffed, as if both of her sons had offended her. "I'm only trying to look out for a woman who has had more than her share of troubles. A woman with a kind heart, at that. Not a lot of those around."

She pointedly looked at Nick, and he knew she was referring to Edie, his ex-wife. It was one thing he and his mother completely agreed on. "Believe me, Mama, hurting Becca is the last thing I want to do. And I'll make sure she does okay."

He was graced by a loving smile. "You're a good boy, Nicky. Now, if you'd just say she can come to the party…"

Somehow his mother had managed to steer the conversation back to where she wanted it, and caught him in her web. He'd lost the battle. It was time for the white flag, before he or Tony blurted out the whole story.

"If that's what you want, Mama, it's okay with me." It took some effort, but he managed to hold back the sigh of defeat that rose in his chest.

THE NEXT MORNING, Nick made a point to pretend nothing had happened between Becca and him the day before. But deep inside, he knew he had taken advantage of an innocent moment. It was his fault, and she had no reason to apologize as she had. He was the one who owed *her* an apology. He just wasn't sure how to go about it.

"Ready, boss?" Clint said, sticking his head inside the trailer.

"One sec," Nick answered, grabbing the coat he had tossed to the chair when he walked in.

"'Morning, Becca," Clint greeted her.

"Good morning, Clint."

"That's a good color on you. Brings out your eyes."

She looked down and tugged at the bottom of her sweatshirt, blushing. "Why, thank you, Clint."

Nick, zipping his down jacket, gritted his teeth. What was with the familiarity between his two best employees?

"Your first interview is at one, Nick," Becca reminded him.

He nodded. "If I'm not here ten minutes before, give me a shout." Grabbing his hat, he turned to Clint. "Lots going on today. Let's get going."

Stepping outside and down to the ground, Nick wondered what this day would bring. Surely it wouldn't be as bad as the day before. Becca had set up all the appointments needed to interview more men for the crew, and he had all of his distributors lined up. He had called each and every one, knowing how much they would appreciate the personal touch.

"Nice lady."

Nick looked at his foreman, walking beside him. "Yeah."

"Pretty, too."

Nick looked at the man closer and narrowed his eyes. "You're a married man, Clint," he reminded him.

"Doesn't mean I can't appreciate a good-looking woman," he answered with a grin. "And aren't you bein' a little touchy?"

Not wanting to discuss his past relationship or even his current one, whatever it was, with Becca, he grunted. "Am I?" But he knew he was, and he needed to fix that.

At a quarter to one, Clint reminded him that he was

supposed to go to the office. Nick thanked him and headed up to the job trailer.

As he opened the door, he heard voices and guessed that the applicant had arrived early. He had hoped he would be in his office before that happened.

He was wrong. About everything.

The newly hired Luke was standing toe-to-toe with Becca, who stood bent backward over her desk, her hands beside her on the edge of it.

"Anytime," Luke was saying. "Just pick up the phone and give me a call."

As Luke attempted to slip a piece of paper into the neck of her sweatshirt, Nick saw red. "Get out, Luke," he said through gritted teeth, keeping his voice low.

Luke stepped back with a swagger and a wide grin on his face. "I was just getting to know the little lady better."

"I said, get out. You'll get your final check in the mail next week."

"Now wait a minute—"

Nick knew he was losing the fine hold he had on his temper. Luke's cocky smile pushed him even closer to the edge, along with the deer-in-the-headlights look on Becca's face.

"No, no minute. Not even a second. You're gone. As of right now." It took a moment before he realized he was shouting. At the same time, he noticed that he had taken his now-former worker by the back of his jacket and was propelling him toward the door.

Clint stood just outside the trailer, watching. "I'll see that he leaves the property with what he came on it with."

Nick slammed the door on the two men outside and

turned to see Becca, still in the same spot, as if frozen to the desk.

"Just what do you think you were doing?" he bellowed.

She shrank back, but couldn't get away. "I wasn't doing anything. He—"

"I know what he was doing," he said, cutting her off without hearing what she was trying to say. "And I know what you were doing. Do you enjoy leading guys on? Is that it? Like you did to me ten years ago?"

He barely noticed how pale she had become, and when he did, he realized what he had said to her.

Too late to take the blurted, angry words back, he wondered what, if anything, he could say that would stop the tears that filled her eyes. At that moment, he hated himself.

Everything happened too fast. Instantly, she was at the door, grabbing her coat from the hook on the wall. "My family will get by somehow; I don't need this job."

"Becca, wait. I didn't mean it. Please. Let me—"

But she was out the door, slamming it behind her.

Chapter Six

Blinded by her tears, Becca managed to jerk open the door of her car and climb inside. For a moment, now that she was alone and out of the line of fire from Nick, she was able to breathe. And think. And even stop crying. She knew she couldn't drive in the state she was in, but neither could she sit in the lot of the construction site. She had to at least drive a few blocks away.

Automatically reaching beside her for her purse, she froze. Her purse wasn't there. She groaned her frustration. In her haste to escape Nick's verbal attack, she had forgotten it. And her keys were in her purse.

Another wave of tears threatened and she gave in to them.

Why was it that whenever she thought things were going well, something had to come along and spoil them? Why was it that—

Beside her, the car door was yanked open and a cold blast of air assaulted her.

"Move over."

When she didn't move, Nick nudged her. "Please," he begged, "just move over and let me in."

She scrambled across the console into the other

bucket seat. She was no match for Nick Morelli, in any way.

She heard him take a deep breath, but she refused to look his way. The tears had halted abruptly the moment he opened the door. She wouldn't shed another. At least not when he could see.

He thrust her purse at her, but not before taking out her car keys. Starting the car, he drove it out of the lot and out onto the street. While his attention was on the road ahead, Becca took a moment to glance at him. His mouth was set in a thin, grim line. She wasn't sure what to make of it and remained silent. What could she say? For almost a week they had managed to skirt around a past they both obviously wanted to forget. But now it was out. At least part of it.

They drove several blocks toward the edge of town, until he turned onto a side street and pulled over. Switching off the engine, he sat staring straight ahead out the windshield.

"I don't know what to say," he said, breaking the silence that filled the interior of the car.

She knew exactly how he felt. Hadn't she been the same just two days ago? She couldn't look at him, but she felt him turn to her.

"I didn't mean a word of it, Becca, I swear. Not one word."

She couldn't answer him. There was nothing she could say to fix it.

"I was angry. Not with you, with him. And, like a fool, I took it out on you. It wasn't fair. It was wrong. *I* was wrong."

She still couldn't speak and simply nodded to let him know she was listening.

"Saying I'm sorry isn't enough, but it's all I have."

It dawned on her that maybe she deserved every word

he had said to her. The way in which she had broken up with him had been heartless. She had known it at the time, but it was the only way she could walk away from what they had. The only way she could keep him from asking too many questions with answers that would hurt him. How many times throughout the past ten years had she wished she could have taken back her words?

Lowering her head so he couldn't see her face, she finally spoke. "Nick—"

"No, don't say it. I won't leave this car until you promise to come back to work. You need this job, Becca. I know you do."

"I think it's time—" she ventured, finally able to look at him.

But he was staring ahead again and didn't notice. "Don't think of me or you. Think of your kids."

She didn't need to. She needed to speak her mind, even if he didn't want to hear her. "Nick, stop. Let me talk."

He ducked his head like a little boy caught with his hand in the cookie jar. "Sorry, I'm just—"

"And *I* have something to tell you."

He looked at her then, and instead of speaking, he nodded, looking as if whatever she was about to say would be the death of him.

It was hard to return his gaze, but she did. "I owe you an apology, too. The other day, when I…I *launched* myself at you, I wasn't thinking. I was so happy to learn that I'd been given an extension on vacating the house, and I just… Well, I lost my head. Maybe like you just did?"

There. It was out in the open. She didn't want to bring up the past, although she knew she owed him an apology for that, too. Now just didn't seem the time. Maybe some-day she could.

He simply looked at her in silence. She couldn't read anything from his expression. Had she, once again, said the wrong thing? But how could it be wrong?

"I'll accept your apology, if you'll accept mine," he finally said. "And come back to work."

Relief swept through her and she smiled as she began to relax. "I accept."

He returned the smile before starting the car and driving back to the site. When they arrived, he pulled up in front of the job trailer and left the motor running. He got out, closed the door and motioned for her to roll down the window. She did as he bid, scooting back into the driver's seat.

He leaned down, holding her with his gaze. "Take the rest of the day off. With pay. Just be here Monday morn-ing, okay?"

She glanced at her watch. "What about your appoint-ments?"

"I can take care of things for one afternoon."

"Of course, you're right."

But there was one more thing she wanted to ask before the opportunity passed her by. She just wasn't sure how to go about it, knowing it could be a risk to open up the past for scrutiny. Finally, she decided to simply say it. "Could we just put the past behind us, Nick? Pretend that we—you and I—don't have a history?"

He studied her for a moment, as if he were remember-ing the same things she was. "That might be pretty hard to do, considering."

He had accepted her apology for throwing herself at

him, and she had accepted his for throwing the past in her face. She wanted so badly to move on with her life, but her guilt about the past—about everything—held her back. She wouldn't ask him to forgive her for what happened ten years ago. It was unforgivable. But they both needed to put it behind them.

"We can try," she said, thinking all he needed was some encouragement. "It would make it so much easier for me to work for you and for us to be friends."

"Friends? I thought we already were."

She sighed and shook her head, seeing that he didn't understand. "I don't mean we aren't. What I mean is, well, friends, not…"

"Former lovers?"

She felt her face grow hot. *Lovers* wasn't exactly the correct term, but it was close enough and she wouldn't argue it. "Yes," she answered in what sounded like a croak.

He looked away and shrugged. "If that's what you want."

She couldn't tell how he felt about her suggestion. "It's not that I want it, but if your wife should—"

"My wife?" He stared at her. "Is that what this is about?"

"No, of course not, but—"

He reached into the car and pressed a finger against her lips. At the same time, he tilted her head up, forcing her to look at him. "Listen and listen well. My wife won't be joining me, if that's what you're afraid of. We've been divorced for several years."

Her mouth formed an O, but nothing came out.

He left her staring after him, her car still running, as a shiver shook her.

"Why aren't you ready to go?"

Becca, dressed in her oldest pair of jeans, complete with patches, waved Raylene into the house and asked, "Go?"

Shaking her head, Raylene walked inside and perched on the arm of the sofa. "Are you trying out for the role of Long John Silver's parrot?"

Becca stared at her, trying to make sense of her friend's comment. "I'm sorry, but I don't understand a word you're saying."

With a dramatic sigh, Raylene shook her head. "The Christmas gala, remember? I said I'd pick you and the kids up at five on Saturday. It's Saturday." She looked at her watch. "And it's five minutes past five."

"I forgot. I'm sorry." Becca picked up April's coat and added it to the other two small ones waiting to be put away under the stairs.

"Okay, you're forgiven. Just hurry up. We don't want to miss the tree lighting."

Becca turned to look at her, badly wanting her friend to go away. "No, what I meant was that I'm sorry you came all the way out here." Continuing to pick up misplaced items, she circled around her friend.

Raylene stepped in front of her, hands on hips, a stubborn gesture she made when there was something she felt needed to be said. "No way are you backing out of this. You told me Sunday, before Nick hired you, that you'd go."

"I told you that I'd try."

"I don't see you trying."

"I don't see any reason why I should, except that you want me to."

Raylene backed up, dropping her hands to her sides.

"What's wrong with you? I know what *was* wrong, but all of a sudden you're—you're…"

Becca had turned to walk away, but she spun to face her again. "I'm what?"

Raylene threw up her hands. "I don't know, Becca. You're afraid?" Turning around, she walked to the door and stopped. "Is that it?" she asked, facing Becca again. "You holed yourself up out here after the divorce, cut yourself off from everyone but me. You won't even make the effort to get out among people who honestly like you and care about you."

Becca had to admit to herself that fear was what held her back. Fear of what people were saying about her, about the end of her marriage. And then as time went on and she ran out of money by making sure every bill from the marriage was paid, she couldn't face them. What had they thought? Poor Becca? Poor little rich girl with nothing to show for it?

"I don't want their pity," she said, her voice trembling with emotions she didn't want to feel.

"All they want to give you is their friendship, hon."

Becca considered it. Could it be true? She had barely spoken with any of them since her divorce. A few had called, but she couldn't face the questions they would ask. Could they really be interested in still being friends with her?

But there was another reason she didn't want to go to the gala. It was where she and Nick had gone on their first date, and it had taken several years before she had been able to attend another one. She thought she'd triumphed over it—had even joined the committee in the first place to flaunt it in the face of her past.

But didn't she want to put the past behind her? Wasn't that what she had asked Nick to do?

"All right," she said, giving in. "I'll go. But on one condition. We split up once we get there."

The smile that appeared on Raylene's face when Becca relented vanished. "Why?"

"Because if people really care, I want to know that it's me, not because of you. Deal?"

Raylene gave a curt nod. "Deal. Whatever it takes to prove it to you."

Becca tried hard for a brave smile, but she knew it was weak, at best. "Then help me get the kids ready to go while I change."

They made it into Katyville before the tree-lighting ceremony began, and after finding a parking spot, the two parted ways. Thanks to the generosity of a few people, Becca was able to move up near the front row of the crowd gathered around the towering tree in the park. Several people greeted her as she passed by them, and she settled in with Danny and her two girls, feeling somewhat better.

Carols were sung, and Becca listened to the young voices of her two oldest children, surprised at how well Danny could sing and that April knew the words to so many songs, even though some were garbled. She was also noticing how less shy her daughter had become and how she had begun to talk more since staying with Gabby. Even in only a week's time, she would chatter away, talking about her best friend, Cat.

When the ceremony was over, Becca kept a tight hold on her children as they weaved their way through the dispersing crowd. A few short blocks away, Katyville's main street had been turned into a winter wonderland, with lights of all colors twinkling to the sound of "The Nutcracker" being piped through a sound system that could be heard throughout most of the small town. As always, there was a bazaar consisting of small booths lining both sides of the street for nearly two blocks. Danny and April tugged at her, eager to see what trinkets were being offered, as she shifted baby Daisy to her other arm.

"Becca? It is you!"

She turned to see an old friend smiling broadly at her. "Hello, Marilyn," she said, surprised.

"My goodness, these kids have grown. And is this the baby? She's beautiful! But of course, she would be."

"Thank you."

"We missed you this year at the gala planning," Marilyn said. "Raylene told us you were busy with the kids, but it just wasn't the same without you. You always have such wonderful ideas to share. Please say you'll be back soon."

"I'll certainly try, but I'm working now—" She suddenly found herself being hugged by another friend.

"Becca! Raylene said you'd be here, but I told her I wouldn't believe it until I saw you." Leaning closer, the woman squinted her eyes and peered at her. "Is it really you?" she asked, and laughed

Becca laughed, too, and nodded. "Yes, Jen, it's me."

"Oh, can I hold her?" she asked, reaching out to Daisy.

Relieved to give her shoulders and arms a short rest, Becca handed Daisy to Jen. Beside her, Danny tugged at her coat.

"Can we get some cocoa?" he asked.

"Of course. In just a few minutes."

Marilyn leaned down to him. "And don't forget

roasted chestnuts. You have to have some of them."
Straightening, she turned to Becca. "We took your idea
after last year's gala and set up tables and chairs in the
parking lot of the bank. Why don't we all go over there
and catch up?"

"Perfect," Jen agreed. "I told my mom to meet me there
later. She has my kids for the duration. Bless her."

All three women laughed at the truth in the statement
and started walking toward the bank. Daisy seemed to be
content in Jen's arms, surprising Becca. Gabby, again, was
the one to thank for that.

Danny pointed out the booth where the hot cocoa was
being sold, and Becca stopped to purchase some for the
three of them, cautioning both him and April not to spill and
to wait until they found a spot to sit before trying to drink it.

Once they were seated, she began to relax, and the three
women talked, while the kids tried out the chestnuts Marilyn bought for them. Except for Raylene, Becca hadn't
spoken with any of her friends since before her divorce,
more than six months ago, before Daisy had been born.
Maybe Raylene had been right, and she shouldn't have
dropped out of sight. Maybe, just maybe, her friends
understood.

"I just love 'The Nutcracker,'" Jen said. "It's so beautiful."

"It wouldn't be Christmas without it," Marilyn agreed.

Becca nodded as Daisy reached out for her. Taking her
baby daughter, she settled back in her chair. "I listen to it
all year long, but I couldn't survive if I couldn't hear it at
Christmastime. Someday, when my girls are older, I'll take
them to see the ballet."

"Oh, they'll enjoy it, Becca," Marilyn said. "I took Samantha when she was six, and I heard nothing else for a year except how much she wanted to be a ballerina."

Becca was envious. It seemed so long since she had been able to give her kids the little extras. Maybe now that she was working, she would be able to start doing that again.

She was enjoying herself so much, she didn't notice Nick emerge from the crowd, until she heard him talking to her son a few feet away from her.

"So what do you think of them?" he asked.

"They're sweet. I like them," Danny replied, taking a drink of his cocoa.

"I've made things from the wood from chestnut trees," Nick said. "I'll have to show them to you."

"Really? That would be neat!"

Nick's hand rested on Danny's shoulder, and Becca felt a tug on her heart. The tug was even harder when he reached out to tickle April, who giggled with glee. It was strange to be here with Nick here, too. But she pushed the memory aside, concentrating instead on what he was saying to Danny.

"That wood is hard to get," Nick went on, while Becca continued to eavesdrop. "There aren't a lot of chestnut trees in this country, and the wood has to be ordered from other countries. But it's good wood, so it's worth it."

"I like trees," April piped up. "Wanna swing in the tree."

"You do, huh?" Nick asked, turning to her and giving her his full attention. "I bet I could make you one."

"Really?"

"Really. When the weather gets warmer, we'll get it done."

Becca smiled, until she remembered that by the time the

weather was warmer, they might not have a tree to hold a swing. They might not have a yard.

"Enjoying yourself?" Nick said, breaking into her thoughts.

Startled, Becca looked up at him, and her heart beat faster. "Why, yes, I am."

"Were you in on the planning of this?" he asked, indicating the entire evening with a slight jerk of his head.

"Not this year. I was…busy."

"But she will be next year," Jen declared. "Good to see you, Nick."

Marilyn nodded. "She always has the best ideas. In fact, these tables are here because she suggested it."

Nick looked at Becca, his expression unreadable. "I'm not surprised."

She felt a warmth flow through her, realizing he was praising her. "They've done a wonderful job without me this year."

Someone called his name, and he excused himself. "I'll see you at the site on Monday, Becca," he said before leaving them.

Jen leaned over the table. "So you *are* working for him. What's it like? He's still as dreamy as ever."

"He's a great boss," Becca answered. "Very nice, very easy to work for."

Marilyn, too, leaned closer. "And very easy on the eyes. But you two know each other," she said with a wink. "Any chance—"

"No," Becca said, wanting to put a stop to any rumors before they began. "We're just friends."

Both women looked disappointed, but the topic was

dropped. A few minutes later, Jen's mother arrived, and soon they had all said their goodbyes to Becca and left with their families.

Becca was thinking of leaving, too, when Nick reappeared with his parents.

"You know my mother and father, don't you, Becca?" he asked.

"Of course," she said, smiling. "It's good to see you both again."

Elena Morelli flashed her a bright smile. "Nick mentioned you were here with your children. I wanted to see them and say hello."

"This is Danny, Mama," Nick said, steering Danny over to his parents, an arm around his shoulder. "Danny, this is my mother, Elena, and my father, Carmine."

Danny quickly ducked his head, but lifted it again. "Hi."

"And this is April." Nick caught her by the waist, as she tried to hide behind her mother, and tickled her. Giggling again, she hid her face in his leg. "She's a little bashful," he told his parents. Turning to Becca, he chucked Daisy under the chin. "And this is Daisy."

Becca could see the yearning in Elena's eyes. "Would you like to hold her?" she asked.

"Oh, I'd love to," Elena cried, reaching out.

To Becca's surprise, Daisy gave a toothless grin when Elena took her.

"And the other one, April, is feeling better?" Elena asked. "Gabby said she had the sniffles."

"She's fine now," Becca said, "but I made sure she was dressed warmly for tonight. I don't know what Gabby gave her, but whatever it was, it worked."

Nick laughed. "Mama's miracle drug."

"It's only herbs," Elena explained. "Nothing that would harm."

Nick raised his hand. "I'll verify that. We rarely had a cold take hold when we were kids. Thanks to Mama, we were a pretty healthy bunch."

Becca watched as Nick's father played peekaboo with Daisy and April in turn. It was easy to see why they'd had six children of their own. "How many grandchildren do you two have now?" she asked them.

Elena looked at her, beaming. "Eight beautiful grand-babies. Gabby's two, then there's Angelo's three and Gino's three. And Tony and Beth are expecting this spring, so it'll be nine soon."

"That's wonderful," Becca told her. "And I'm sure you spend a lot of time with them."

Elena nodded. "Except for Angelo's. They live in St. Louis, but they come home every Christmas and visit in the summer. We are a very lucky family."

"Yes, you are," Becca replied. *And very full of love.* She envied them all. They were so unlike her own family, even when her mother was still alive.

Carmine spoke for the first time. "We'd better be going, *cara.*"

"Oh, Carmine," Elena sighed.

"Little ones need their sleep," he told her.

With another heavy sigh, she placed Daisy in Becca's lap. "Come see us," she told Becca. She slid Nick a look that Becca couldn't decipher. "Come to Tony's birthday party. Nick will give you the information."

Becca noticed that Nick opened his mouth as if to say

something to his mother, then immediately closed it again. "We'll see," Becca replied, unsure of what was going on between mother and son.

When the parents were gone, Nick lingered, talking with Danny and April. Becca was glad they were all forming a friendship, but on the other hand, she wasn't sure how good it would be for her children. They needed a male figure in their lives, especially Danny, but why Nick? They would be moving soon, making a friendship difficult, if not impossible.

Checking her watch, she saw that it was time to meet Raylene. She began to gather up her things and sent Danny to dispose of their empty cups and trash. ·

"You're leaving?" Nick asked.

Becca nodded without looking at him. She was still a little uneasy when left alone with him, after what had taken place a couple of days ago. Not that they were really alone in the middle of the Christmas gala crowd. "Raylene picked us up," she explained. "I'm meeting her at the park near the tree."

"I'll walk with you," he said. She looked up at him, and he obviously read the question in her eyes. "You can use an extra pair of hands to corral the kids. And April looks tired. I can carry her."

With no real reason to turn down his offer, Becca simply nodded.

They walked the few blocks in silence, except when Nick explained about his parents. "You remember my mother," he said. "She adores kids, and someone happened to mention that they'd seen you with yours. When she found me, she insisted I find you and take her to you."

"It's okay, Nick. Your mother is a wonderful person. I'm glad I got to see her. Daisy took right to her, and your father, too."

"Yeah, she did."

Silence fell between them once again, and Becca was relieved. The last thing she wanted to do was rehash their conversation from the other day. Enough had been said.

Raylene was waiting at the brightly lit Christmas tree when they reached the park. Becca was proud when her best friend only greeted Nick and said little else. Sometimes Raylene spoke before thinking, but tonight she was more sensible. Maybe she sensed Becca's mood.

"So?" Raylene asked as they drove out of town. "How did it go? Was I right?"

Becca chuckled. Raylene loved being right. "Yes, you were." And she was glad. She'd been a fool to keep herself away from her friends and neighbors because she was ashamed. She'd never had anything to be ashamed of.

Tonight, she had many things to be thankful for. Good friends, a job she liked, children she loved. Life was beginning to look up. The future didn't look as bleak as it had even a week ago. It was the past that still made her uncomfortable, but she had made it through the evening, in spite of that. Someday, she would even battle those demons and win.

Chapter Seven

Nick held tight to the door of the job trailer as he eased it open. The wind had kicked up overnight, bringing colder weather that hinted at snow, and he didn't want to let in any more cold air than he had to. The job trailer was just that— a trailer. And an old one and small one, at that. Insulation was nearly nonexistent, and the heat was sometimes iffy. He hoped Becca had dressed with the weather in mind. The crew would be wandering in after lunch for their paychecks, and the interior of the trailer could easily be freezing before the end of the day, if the temperature continued to drop.

Slipping inside quickly, he closed the door behind him and immediately caught sight of Becca. She was looking even prettier than usual in a blue sweater. "Cold today," he commented, needing something to say as he peeled off his coat and gloves.

Becca placed a stapler on a pile of papers the small gust of wind had caught. "Yes, it is. Looks like winter has finally arrived. And here I was hoping we'd continue with the decent weather." She looked up at Nick with a wry smile. "Decent for the middle of December, that is."

He shrugged. "It's Kansas. Tomorrow could be in the seventies."

On her way to the coffeemaker, she laughed. "So they say, but I'll believe it when I see it."

As had become his habit since hiring her, he watched her pour a mug of coffee for him. "You know, you don't have to do this. I *can* make coffee," he said, taking the mug from her.

Her face paled. "Is it that bad?"

"Hell— I mean, no way! It's dam— It's good coffee." He ducked his head, took a sip of the hot drink and murmured, "Sorry."

"Don't worry about it," she said, laughing. "I've heard worse. There's no reason to tiptoe around me. I've occasionally said a few choice words of my own."

He watched her pour a mug of coffee for him, then waited as she settled behind the desk and thought about how well she fit in with the operations of the company. He'd hate to lose her. But lose her, he would, in more ways than one, when she learned who her new landlord was. The old saying "Hell hath no fury" came to mind.

Not wanting to deal with it until he had to, he turned his mind to business. "Trudy will be here soon with payroll checks. I'll need to sign them, so bring them on into my office."

"I'm looking forward to meeting your bookkeeper," Becca replied.

"She's a good one. I was lucky to find her."

"She works out of her home?"

He nodded. "I think you'll like her. You two have a lot in common. She's a single mom, too."

Becca tilted her head to the side and studied him. "You have a talent for rescuing women."

The remark made him uncomfortable. She had no idea just how much rescuing he had done when it came to her. "Not as much as you might think."

She smiled as if she didn't believe him. When the phone rang, she answered it, and he took the opportunity to escape to his office. What she didn't know wouldn't hurt her—he hoped—but now that he thought about it, it could very well hurt him.

He was the cause of her heartache.

He knew in his heart that he should tell her the truth and should have from the beginning. Looking back, being honest would have been easier. And tell her, he would. But not right now. He hadn't figured out the best way to do it with the least amount of fallout.

He was a man who planned in great detail, but he hadn't planned on running into Becca and meeting her kids or learning that she was on the brink of losing her home— and that his dreams were the cause of it. Because of them, he had acted rashly, and now he was paying the price.

He was deep in thought about how to extricate himself from his problem when he heard a soft knock on his door. "Come in," he called.

Becca stepped inside the office and up to his desk with the payroll checks in hand. "You said to bring them to you immediately. And you were right. Trudy is very nice."

Taking them from her, he nodded. "I knew you'd like her. I'll get these signed right away, and they'll be available after—" He glanced at his watch and was surprised that the morning was nearly gone already. "Noon is the usual time, so I'd better get busy."

"Leave them alphabetized," she said, before leaving him to his work.

He smiled when she was gone. Who was the boss, anyway?

Just as he finished signing the last of the checks, his foreman arrived with a new problem, and Nick followed him outside to deal with it. But before he left his office, he pulled the envelope marked with Becca's name from the others and stuck it in his pocket.

Two hours later, the problem solved, Nick was eager to get inside, out of the cold and wind. He had cautioned his men to dress warmly and stay out of the harsh wind as much as possible. With Becca's help, he also offered hot coffee in the office for those who either didn't have a thermos or had run out. The safety and health of his crew was important. Without them, his company wouldn't exist.

Becca was busy handing out paychecks to two of his men when he returned to the trailer, and he had started down the narrow hallway to his office when he realized he still had her paycheck in his pocket. Backtracking, he waited while she finished her business and the men had gone before pulling out the envelope.

"This belongs to you," he said. He walked to her desk, where she stood, and handed it to her. "I wanted to give it to you myself." Realizing how that might sound, he added a shrug. "New employee, and all that."

She took it from him and looked at it. "Mine?" she asked. When he nodded, she slowly turned it over in her hands and opened it. As she pulled out the check, her eyes widened and she looked closer at it. "This much for a week?"

When she glanced up at him, he saw the surprise in her eyes, and he nodded. "I pay well. Relatively, anyway."

She stared at it, and then sank to her chair. "I hadn't expected—"

This time, when she looked up at him, her eyes sparkled with joy. It was worth taking his mother's suggestion and increasing Becca's pay, if only a little. "First paycheck, huh?" he asked, unable to hide his smile.

Her answering nod changed to slow head-shaking. "I don't know what to say."

"There's nothing to say. You earned it."

"Wow." It came out as a whisper.

He was enjoying this as much as he had thought he would. Maybe even more. Perching on the edge of her desk across from her, he laughed. "I remember my first paycheck. Of course, it was just a written check from Bill Watkins, but I knew I'd earned every penny of it."

She gave him a questioning look, and he explained. "He needed some brush cleared from the pasture. That was back when he still did a little of his own farming. He'd asked Johnny Grayson and Lou Harrelson to do it. Do you remember them?"

"Sure," she answered. "Johnny still lives here, and Lou's in Wichita."

He nodded and then chuckled to himself. "Well, I'd been needing a new tire for my bicycle. Pop had told me that I'd have to find a way to pay for it myself. I was, what…? Maybe seven or eight? And I begged them to let me help. I finally convinced them that I could work as hard as they could, in spite of me being inches shorter and fairly scrawny."

"You were never scrawny, Nick."

"Oh, yeah, I was. When I was really young."

"So your first paying job was clearing brush for Bill Watkins."

Her eyes were dreamy, as if her thoughts were drifting back to the past, and he, too, was thinking of that day and feeling his excitement at the opportunity to earn the money he needed. "I worked my rear end off. More than the other two—or at least *I* thought so. And I was worn out when Watkins handed me the check. But I don't think I was ever so proud of anything in my life."

Her smile stretched into a grin. "Well, I may not be seven or eight, and I have to admit that I enjoy doing what I'm doing, but I know how you must have felt."

Their gazes held for several seconds, until he noticed a blush coloring her cheeks, and she looked away as if embarrassed.

"What do you plan to do with it?" he asked, indicating the check still in her hand.

"Pay bills, of course," she answered, as if he thought she would spend it on a cruise or something.

But he'd had a flicker of an idea as he'd signed her check, and he needed a way to implement it. "Sure," he said, "but you'll have another check next week, so you wouldn't have to pay everything with this one."

"Well… I suppose I could…"

"Christmas is only two weeks away," he went on. "If you wait until the last minute, you might not be able to find what you want."

She smiled. "You do have a point. Although I don't plan to spend a lot. Responsibilities come first."

"Spread those out. If a bill isn't due this week, pay it next week. Responsibility and enjoyment should be balanced. Otherwise, life's a drag." He was itching to buy a few things for Danny, April and Daisy, and he wanted to get her take on what he was thinking of buying. She wasn't nearly as excited at the thought of shopping than he had expected her to be. Instead, she was proving exactly how responsible and levelheaded she was. He wasn't entirely disappointed, considering the way Edie had thought money was something to spend on any and all extravagances.

By the doubtful look on her face, it was clear she needed convincing. "I have nieces and nephews to buy for. I've been putting it off, not sure what to get them. I was hoping you would help."

"You're right about the bills," she admitted. "I've never had a steady, regular income, so I don't know what it's like. Not to mention it would be fun to help buy for your nieces and nephews, so…a little Christmas shopping, it is."

He got to his feet before she could change her mind. "I'll call Gabby and make sure she can watch your kids for a while longer. We can leave right after work."

"I'll have to put gas in my car."

He shook his head. "I'll drive." He wasn't going to debate with her. It was his plan, no matter how quickly conceived, and he would see it carried through, in spite of her obvious doubts. "We can leave from here, do the shopping, grab a bite to eat and then I'll bring you back here to your car."

"So I don't have a say in it?" Her lips trembled with the smile she tried to hide.

"No. No say at all."

Laughing, she shook her head. "Nick, you're incorrigible."

He studied her. "Not a rescuer, after all, huh?"

"That, too."

"Okay, if you say so. Then it's all settled."

"DANNY NEEDS CLOTHES, Nick, much more than toys." But judging by the stubborn look on his face, Becca wasn't going to win this argument.

"Christmas isn't Christmas without a few toys," he reminded her.

The mall was crowded with shoppers, and Becca was tired. She had debated buying new coats for her little ones, but wasn't sure how she could stretch to afford them and pay the bills she owed. Stores in the mall were expensive, but luckily, she had found some sales. Unfortunately, coats weren't among them.

She made a point to look at the number of bags Nick was holding. "You may not have a problem spoiling those nieces and nephews, but I know what's best for my own kids."

Nick blew out a frustrated sigh. "I'm not saying you don't. It's your choice what you give them, but I want to give them something, too. And before you say that I don't need to, remember that I said I *want* to."

Determined not to lose this round, she gave in, but with reservations. "All right. One gift each, under ten dollars."

"Fifteen."

She considered it. "Deal."

"My choice?"

"Your choice."

Feeling better now that they both were somewhat satisfied, she wandered into a shoe store. "I'm only window-shopping," she told him over her shoulder. Her ex-husband had hated shopping with her, and she didn't want Nick to think she was wasting his time. "Just for a few minutes."

He followed without complaint and shrugged. "Everybody needs shoes, especially this time of year. Barefoot just doesn't get it."

She was surprised at how casually he reacted, and she stopped for a moment to look at a pair of fur-lined boots. They would certainly come in handy, especially in the office. The wind coming in earlier that day had nearly frozen her ankles, even though she was wearing jeans and long socks.

"How about these?" he asked from behind her.

She turned to see him holding a pair of sexy black heels with tiny straps. They were lovely, and she was tempted to try them on, even though she knew she couldn't buy them. Shoes—especially pretty, dressy ones—had always been one of her weaknesses. But instead of giving in, she shook her head. "Not so good for cold weather and snow."

"But for something fun—"

"I don't have anywhere to wear something like that," she admitted. She hated to say it, but she had to. "I have to be practical."

"Right. And we're only looking." With what she read as reluctance, he returned the shoes to the shelf.

"They are nice, though," she said, wondering if she had sounded like an old stick-in-the-mud.

Nick apparently understood. "I was taught that we couldn't always have what we want and that there's no sense in buying something we wouldn't use. With six kids in the family, it wasn't hard to learn why."

Being the only child of parents who could buy much of what she wanted, Becca hadn't been brought up with the same standards Nick had, but she had learned them quickly over the past year. "It wouldn't hurt for most people to learn that," she agreed.

As they left the store, she thought back over her childhood. She hadn't wanted for a lot, and she had known at an early age that if she wanted it, more than likely it would be given to her. The one thing she had wanted, she had gotten by hook and by crook, sneaking out with the help of her best friend to see Nick. He was the one thing her father hadn't allowed her. Nick had never measured up to her father's idea of the right man for her.

Stealing a glance at him, she smothered a sigh. It was too bad her father couldn't see the man Nick was now.

In only the few minutes they'd been in the shoe store, the crowd in the mall had worsened. Becca was jostled by people working their way from one side of the wide walkway to the other, and she held tight to her purchases. She was nearly knocked off her feet as three teenagers bulled their way through the crowd, and she felt Nick take hold of her arm.

"I'm sorry. Excuse me," a voice behind her said. Recognizing it, she froze. Not now, she prayed. *Not here.*

HOLDING TIGHT TO BECCA, Nick glared after the unruly kids who had nearly run her down. He felt her stiffen, heard a man say her name and turned toward the sound of the voice. Becca pulled away from him, and he saw the man who had spoken to her.

"Hello, Jason," she said.

He appeared uncomfortable, unable to look right at her. When he smiled, it was easy to see that it was forced. "How are you, Becca?" he asked.

"I'm good," she said, offering her own small smile. Sensing something wasn't right, Nick moved closer. Becca looked up at him, the same smile still on her face, before turning to the man. "Jason, this is Nick Morelli. Nick, Jason Tyler."

Tyler? But that was Becca's last name. Who— Nick gave her a questioning look.

"Jason is my ex-husband."

Without feeling the least bit shy, Nick looked him over. So this was the guy who left his three kids behind. He obviously wasn't concerned with their welfare, and, by the look of the woman with him, was adding to the mix with another kid. She was definitely pregnant and looked ready to…*pop* was the word that came to mind.

Switching the bags in his right hand to his left, Nick stuck out his free hand to Jason, while he slipped his other around Becca's waist, bags and all. "Nice to meet you, Jason," he said, as if he might like the man, and added a friendly smile.

Jason must have noticed Nick's glance at the woman, because he looked at her, then at Becca. "My wife, Devra," he said.

Nick noticed that Becca greeted her with her usual friendliness, and he marveled at it. If the shoe had been on the other foot, he wouldn't have been so nice.

"We've been shopping for the kids," Nick announced, holding up his bounty of bags from behind Becca. He doubted Jason had been doing the same. Then he shifted to the other side of her to slip his right hand around her waist. She moved an inch away, but he held her steady. He had a feeling she needed some support. And if her ex wanted to think there was something going on, Nick didn't care at all. In fact—

"Did you say Morelli?" Jason asked.

"Yes," Nick answered. It was an old habit, but he was prepared to defend his family name by pointing out exactly who he was and what he did.

"Big Sky Construction Morelli?"

It seemed he wouldn't have to defend anything, after all. "Yes. That's my company."

Jason's eyes widened. "Impressive. I've heard Big Sky is the fastest-growing construction company in Colorado."

"We're here in Kansas, now."

"Really? Based here in Wichita?"

Nick had to hold back a smile. "In Katyville."

At the news, Jason's eyebrows shot up, and he looked to Becca. "That's interesting." Focusing again on Nick, he said, "You're part of the Katyville Morellis then?"

Nick had known better than to let down his guard. "That's my family, yes. You may have had work done on your car in Katyville. My brother owns that business now, passed down from my father."

"He's a good mechanic," Jason said, nodding, although it didn't appear that he was pleased to admit it. "One of the best in the area."

Nick let loose with a smile. It was hard not to feel smug, but at least the guy was good enough not to lie about it. Not that it earned Jason Tyler any points for fatherhood, and that was Nick's biggest beef.

He wished he knew more about Becca's marriage to the guy and what had happened for it to end in divorce. Not to mention the relationship they had, now that it was over. He knew Danny hadn't had any attention from his father but there wasn't a lot that could be done about the past, except to make amends in the present. Whether Becca wanted him to or not, he intended to help with those.

Becca's voice pulled him from his thoughts. "It was nice meeting you," she was saying to the new wife. Nick didn't detect a bit of anything negative in her voice.

After saying their goodbyes, she slipped out of his hold and turned to look up at him. "Thank you," she said. "Again."

Nick's heart skipped a beat at the shimmer in her eyes. "No need to thank me. I didn't do anything."

"Yes, you did."

She turned and walked away, leaving Nick behind, and he hurried to catch up to her. He wanted to continue the conversation, but he sensed she didn't. "Look, divorce is tough. It can leave a person feeling raw. But I have to say I admire the way you handled running into them."

She shrugged one shoulder, but didn't look at him. "Bearing a grudge does no good. To be honest, it's easier just to think of him as someone I once knew and leave it at that. Of course, it doesn't mean I wasn't in a state of shock to suddenly have him standing there."

Nick wasn't sure how to take that, and he had to admit it hurt a little. Becca had managed to break his heart once, and he wouldn't let it happen again. "So that's the way it is with me, too? I'm just someone you once knew?"

Lowering her head, she shook it, but Nick didn't catch what she was saying. Bending down, he asked her to repeat it.

"It's not the same. Not at all," she answered.

Straightening, he stared at the crowd around them, rushing to finish their Christmas shopping. But he saw nothing. He was trying to figure out what she meant. Was it good? Or was it bad?

"We really need to talk about this sometime," he finally managed to say.

She simply nodded, but she didn't suggest a time and place. That would obviously be Nick's job. And he definitely wasn't going to let it pass.

Chapter Eight

Feeling as if someone was watching him, Nick looked up from the paperwork on his desk to find Becca standing in the open doorway of his office.

"Is there something I can help you with?"

Her hesitation and the look of ambivalence on her face made him wonder if her ex might be causing problems. It had been two days since they'd had the run-in at the mall, and Becca hadn't mentioned a word about it.

He got up from the desk and moved a stack of papers from the only other available chair in the room. "Come sit down and tell me what it is."

She gave him a tentative smile and took the seat he offered. "This is probably none of my business."

"No harm in trying."

Taking a deep breath, she folded her hands in her lap. "After batting zero in the apartment search, so far, I started thinking. This housing development you're working on—"

"*We're* working on," he corrected.

That brought another smile. "*We're* working on. Well, it's great, but it's for upper-middle-class families. There are so many new homes being built around the area, I keep wondering if a lot of people, who have just as great a need for a new home, wouldn't benefit from a smaller-scaled project."

She let out a breath, and he realized how nervous she was talking about it. He wasn't sure if asking this question might be harder than answering it. Add that to how she had rushed through the last part of it, and he was sure she had been rehearsing every word of it. At least she had the courage to ask.

"I definitely see your point," he said, settling in his chair behind his desk again. "But I'm not a builder, not a developer, so I don't have a say in what's built." Her shoulders drooped, and he felt bad to be disappointing her. "I don't know of anyone who has any current interest in providing a more...economical project, but I'll keep my ear to the ground."

She got to her feet. "Thanks." Turning, she started for the door, and immediately turned back around. "I guess you wouldn't make as much on a smaller project."

"That's not necessarily my criteria." Although he would have to admit that it helped.

Before he could say more, the phone rang. She reached to answer it before he did, greeted the caller and pushed the hold button. "It's the blueprint company. The revised prints are ready."

Nick got to his feet. "I'll go pick them up now."

As Becca relayed the message, Clint came in the door and down the hall. "We got trouble, boss."

As soon as Clint explained the most recent problem, Becca spoke up. "I'll pick up the prints."

"No," Nick said. "It's cold out there and—"

"I have a coat and a heater in my car, and I know

where the place is." Becca squeezed past Clint and started down the hall.

"We need you now, boss," Clint said, when Nick started to follow her. "It may not take long, but…" He shrugged.

Nick slowed his steps but didn't stop moving. "Yeah, I'll be there in a sec."

Becca was pulling on her coat and grabbing her purse. "It won't take long. Can someone keep a watch on the office?"

Nick stood by the door as Clint joined them. "I'll lock up and put a note on the door."

Beside him, Clint nodded. "Won't be the first time nobody was in the office. And you drive careful. Looks like we may get some snow."

"I will."

Nick didn't miss the friendly pat on the arm she gave Clint as she moved past him to the door, and he had to hustle to get it open for her. "Let me know when you get back if I'm not in the trailer," he told her as she hurried to her car.

Waving to let him know she had heard him, she climbed in and started the engine. Nick watched her drive away.

"Give her some room, boss."

"What?" He turned to look at his foreman.

"She's a big girl."

No, she's not, Nick thought, and then had to remind himself that she was a grown woman, even though she needed a little help now and then. "Let's get this problem taken care of. What's going on?"

Ten minutes later, he was unlocking the door to the job trailer, with the problem solved. But the clouds had gathered and it had begun to snow, coming down in huge, thick flakes. Inside, he heard the phone ringing and nearly took the door off its hinges trying to get in, certain it was Becca having trouble of her own.

"What happened?" he barked into the receiver.

"Why, nothing yet," Gabby answered, "but I do need to ask a favor."

Nick relaxed at the sound of her voice. "What is it?"

"I need to take a prescription out to Joe's mom. You know she had hip surgery, and I'm afraid if I don't do it now and this snow keeps up, I might not get it there, especially if there's any wind and drifting."

"And?"

"And I don't want to take three kids and two babies, both napping right now, out in this weather. I need someone to watch them while I take the prescription out. If Becca could—"

"She's on an errand and won't be back for a while. How long will you be?"

"Thirty minutes, tops, if that."

He checked his watch. Becca probably hadn't even made it into Wichita yet, much less gotten to the printer. He could only imagine what a struggle it would be for Gabby to bundle up five kids and load them into her van for a five-minute drive out and another back. Joe's mother lived on the outskirts of Katyville. "As long as you promise not to sit and chitchat with Joe's mom, I'll do it."

After hanging up, he scribbled a note for Becca and left it taped to the outside of the trailer door. He also let Clint know and told him to call him on his cell phone if he was needed and if Becca returned before he did. Then he mentally kicked himself for not giving Becca his cell.

BECCA BLEW ON HER cold fingers and blinked at the snow-flakes falling like a curtain from the sky as she carefully climbed the snow-covered steps into the job trailer.

"It's about time!"

She jerked her head up at the sound of Nick's angry voice. But it wasn't fury that she saw in his eyes. It was worry.

"Did you send the crew home?" she asked, pulling off her knit cap and gloves, and then fumbling with her cold fingers on the buttons of her coat.

"About twenty minutes ago. How bad are the roads?"

She shook her head. "Not good and getting worse."

"Don't take your coat off." He picked up the phone and started punching keys. "I'm going to follow you to Gabby's in my pickup. Just let me give her a call to let her know we're on our way."

"The streets here in town aren't that bad."

He shook his head as he spoke into the phone. "She's here and we're on our way." Replacing the receiver, he turned to face her. "Don't argue. You'll need some help getting the kids in the car, and I intend to follow you home, too."

"The roads home are familiar. I know the bad spots. I'll be fine."

The stubborn set to his jaw told her it would be useless to protest, so she slipped her coat back on her shoulders. "We'll discuss it when we get to Gabby's."

Twenty minutes later, with April and Daisy in Becca's car and Danny in Nick's truck—thanks to Danny's stub-born insistence that he could only ride with Nick—the snow on the ground and streets had deepened. Becca hated driving in it. The only light in the sky was from the streetlights, which glowed like snowy halos as Becca made her way out of Katyville.

The normally ten-to-fifteen-minute drive to her house took them a little over thirty minutes, and more than once, Becca had nearly slid into one of the deep ditches on either side of the dirt road. The snow, whipped by the wind and coming down steadily at an angle, had blinded her, and a chill of fear had kept her fingers in a death grip on the steering wheel. When they finally turned, sliding into her driveway, she was ready to cry from sheer nerves.

Nick, carrying Danny, met her at her car and took April from her. Her nerves still on edge, even now that they were safely home, she reached in and took a sleeping Daisy from her car seat and followed Nick to the house.

After fumbling with the lock, she finally managed to open the door and step inside. Nick followed behind her and placed Danny and April on the sofa.

"It's cold in here," she said, snuggling Daisy closer and flipping on the light.

Nick walked over to the thermostat near the stairway and peered at it. "The furnace must be off. I'll go down and check it out."

"No. Nick, wait. It'll take too long and—" She looked toward the window, where the storm raged outside. With a heavy sigh, she gave in to fate. There was no way she could send Nick home in this kind of weather. "Never mind."

"It'll only take a few minutes. It's a gas furnace, and the wind probably blew out the pilot light," he said, disappearing around the corner.

Becca turned to the two serious little faces of her oldest children huddled on the sofa. "I'll put some leftover soup on to heat, and as soon as you've eaten and it's warm again, you two are off to bed." She expected at least some argument, especially from Danny, but both of them nodded.

"Is Nick going home, Mom?" Danny asked. "Will he be okay out in the snow?"

Becca didn't even want to think about having Nick in her house all night. After the harrowing drive home, she wasn't feeling calm enough to deal with that. But the weather outside didn't look as if it would let up anytime soon, and she didn't see any choice in the matter. "It was a scary drive home, wasn't it?" she asked her son, trying to keep the conversation as normal as possible.

"He shouldn't go."

Becca's eyes stung with tears at the somber look on her son's face. Moving close, she brushed the silky hair from his forehead. "He won't, honey. I won't let him." Turning to April, she noticed her daughter blinking sleep back. "Want to watch a little television? Special treat."

April immediately nodded and snuggled into the pillows on the sofa. Becca turned on the TV and found an appropriate channel, then she took Daisy upstairs and put her to bed. Gabby had fed her before they arrived, so there was a good chance she might sleep through the night.

She didn't see Nick downstairs when she returned and went to the kitchen to warm the soup. Hoping he wasn't having trouble with the furnace, she turned her head at the sound of footsteps behind her. "I hope soup is all right."

Nick sniffed the air. "Smells great, and as much as I'd like to stay and enjoy it, I'd better be heading home."

Placing the spoon on the stove, she faced him. "Nick, you can't—"

"The house should warm up fairly quickly, but if you have some wood, I can start a fire in the fireplace to keep the chill off until it does."

When he started to move away, she reached out and put her hand on his arm. "You can't go home in this, Nick. If anything would happen to you, I—" Her throat closed at the thought, and she couldn't finish.

Nick covered her hand with his, sending a warmth through her that she had thought she would never feel again. "I lived in Colorado for years," he said, his voice low and easy. "I'll be okay, and I have my cell phone. If nothing else, Tony can always get the wrecker out and come get me."

"And then I'd have two of you to worry about. No, you aren't leaving. You'll stay here where I know you're safe and not freezing to death in a snow-filled ditch out there."

She dared to look directly into his eyes and saw something there she wasn't sure she wanted to put a name to. It took all her effort to ward off the hot shiver that shot through her.

"What would people say?" he whispered.

It took her a moment to find her voice. "To hell with them."

Nick's eyes widened in surprise and he stepped back, laughing. "Becca, what language."

The moment was broken, and she laughed, too. "Well, it's true. Your health and life are much more important than what a bunch of gossips would make of you staying. *If* they ever found out."

His eyes softened for a brief second, and then he nodded. "You're right, on all accounts," he conceded. "I'll stay. To tell the truth, I wasn't looking forward to driving back to Katyville in this weather. Is there firewood in the house?"

She turned back to the stove, her hand trembling as she picked up the spoon and stirred the soup, and she hoped he didn't notice. "Only a little. The rest is outside in back, next to the steps. There's a tarp over it, so the snow might have covered it."

"I'll get some now, before it gets worse out there."

"Do I need to tie a rope to your waist?" she asked, as he started for the back door.

He looked back at her with a grin. "I hope it isn't that bad, but keep the light burning in here, just in case."

"No argument from me on that."

BY THE TIME Nick had the fire laid and it was burning to his satisfaction in the fireplace, April and Danny had finished their soup and yawned their way to bed. Even Daisy was tucked away for the night.

He watched Becca descend the stairs, the firelight sending warm shadows her way and flickering gold in her hair.

"So?" he asked when she moved farther into the room.

Her smile was tired. "They're asleep. Apparently it's been quite a day."

Nick started to tell her about his very short time watching over them at Gabby's, but Becca moved on to the dining room.

"Come eat some soup," she called to him, "before it gets cold."

He joined her at the table and filled his bowl, still feeling a slight chill in the air. Apparently, the furnace hadn't yet caught up, and the fire was only warming the space near it. "Would it be against house rules to eat this by the fireplace? There's something about a crackling fire…"

She gave him a measuring look from top to bottom. "I guess you're old enough that I can trust you with a bowl of soup. Sure. Eating by the fire sounds heavenly. Let's do it."

He could think of other things that were heavenly when done by the fire, but they weren't for the two of them. Not now.

While Nick settled onto the raised fireplace hearth, Becca turned off the TV and switched on a nearby radio. "Not much on tonight." Taking two pillows from the sofa, she put them on the floor across from him and dropped onto them. "The radio will probably have better weather reports and no laugh tracks."

"Let me take a guess. The forecast is for snow?"

Becca laughed, the lines around her mouth easing. "Undoubtedly. Will your parents be worried that you aren't there?"

"I called them while you were putting the kids to bed. They said it's a wise decision. I guess that makes you the wise one of the two of us."

Becca turned her head to stare at the fire. "I'm sure you had your reasons for wanting to leave."

Becca might be surprised to find out what he was really feeling. Staying gave them the chance to talk. He hoped that maybe they could open the door a crack to the secrets both of them kept. He suspected she had her share, just as he did. He had come to a place where he wasn't sure about anything, any more than he could put his feelings for her into words. He badly wanted to take a risk with her, but the ghosts of the past wouldn't let him.

If he just knew the truth about what happened ten years ago, it would help him sort things out.

"Maybe you just think you know what those reasons are," he said, taking the leap.

When she didn't move or speak, he hesitated. But the need to get to the heart of it pushed him on. Reaching across the space that separated them, he took her hand in his. "Becca…"

It struck him as a good sign when she didn't pull her hand away, but when she turned to look at him, tears shimmered in her eyes, and he almost called it all to a halt.

"If I had been you, I'd have hated me."

Her words sent his mind tumbling back to the day she told him she wasn't interested in seeing him anymore, and he could still remember the pain he had felt. "If I say I didn't, I'd be a liar," he admitted.

One glistening tear, sparkling with red and gold from the firelight, slowly slid down her cheek as she nodded. "You have every right."

Taking her other hand, he pulled her to her feet and guided her to sit next to him on the hearth. "*Had.* It's in the past."

She shook her head and tried to pull away. "That night you found me on the road with the flat, I could see the memory of what I had done had never gone away. And I'm just— I'm sorry."

Her chin dipped down on the final word, and he couldn't see her face. "That night I found you on the road, I was surprised to see you. No. I was shocked. I suppose I knew we'd run into each other sooner or later. I'd hoped later, because I couldn't imagine what it would be like. And, yeah," he admitted, "I guess there was some lingering resentment, but that has nothing to do with tonight."

He stopped, not sure if he was ready to continue. But if

he didn't do it now, would he miss the one chance he might have? Taking a deep breath, he held on to her hands, hoping she wouldn't pull away. "I meant what I said about people talking. But that wasn't the only reason."

He needed to see her face. Needed to see her eyes to read the truth in them. Raising his hand while still holding hers, he tipped her chin up with his knuckles and gazed into her eyes. And saw fear. He had the sudden urge to run, to hit the door, climb in his truck and drive away. To hell with the snow.

Instead, he said the only thing he could. "What you said to me that day, ten years ago, didn't kill every feeling I had for you. The hate I felt back then was because it hurt so much. After a while, it all went away. And then I saw you on that road in the middle of the night, and it all came back and hit me. Hard. I didn't know how to deal with it. I still don't."

"I didn't want to break up with you, Nick," she said, her voice a soft whisper.

"I think I figured that out, but I never knew for sure."

"My father... It was his idea. But don't blame him," she hurried to add. "He thought he was doing what was best for me."

Nick felt the old resentment threaten, and had to turn away so Becca wouldn't notice. He knew at the time that her father didn't think he was good enough for her. His family hadn't had money. But he had proven the man wrong. *As good as Jock Malone,* had been his mantra. It had gotten him through college. After that, it hadn't mattered. Nick grew up and went on with his life.

"Before the night we broke up, he didn't know I was seeing you."

Nick twisted back to stare at her. "What?"

"I was sneaking around to see you, Nick. I was afraid he wouldn't approve, but I don't think that was the only reason he insisted I break up with you. I knew he was afraid to lose me. He had been so lost when my mother died. I don't think anybody saw it but me. He's a hard man. A very private man. He would never let anyone see his emotions. And then when he found out that I was lying to him about who I was seeing…"

Nick almost found the confession laughable. He had hated her father more and for longer than he had hated her. And he still resented the man.

She took a deep breath. "I knew if I told you my father didn't want me to see you anymore, you wouldn't accept it and would think he believed you weren't good enough. I was afraid it would hurt you even more, so the only thing I could do was to tell you I didn't want to see you anymore. I thought—I *believed* that, given some time, he'd give in or wouldn't care. But you left for college. You didn't come back and I never heard from you. I gave up hope and married Jason, my father's choice. And look what it got me."

Her tears were falling freely now, and Nick gathered her in his arms. All this time…

BECCA AWAKENED slowly to a sunlit room, not yet ready to open her eyes, while luxuriating in warmth and wondering what it was that was making her smile. Sounds drifted to her, little by little, until she realized they were the sounds of Danny and April running in the hallway upstairs.

And then she realized where she was.

"Good morning, sleepyhead."

Her breath caught and she squeezed her eyes shut. She hadn't! She couldn't.

No, of course she hadn't. She knew that. Even if she had wanted to—and from what she remembered in her waking state, the desire wasn't imagined—she felt sure Nick wouldn't have allowed it.

"The kids are up," she said, her voice raspy. Peeling away her side of the blankets covering both of them, she sat up and swung her feet to the living room floor. Her body ached. The sofa was not the place to spend the night, especially when shared with someone. Feeling a chill, she realized that it was because she missed Nick's warmth next to her.

From behind, she felt him shift, and she bit her lip to keep from reaching out to him.

"Go check on them," he said. "I'll rustle up something to eat."

He was up and moving before she was, while she tried to clear the cobwebs from her mind. Before she succeeded, Danny was bounding down the stairs, April close behind.

"Daisy's crying, Mom," he said as he streaked through the living room.

"She wants her bottle," April said, following him.

Relieved to have an excuse to escape before having to face Nick, she hurried up the stairs to tend to Daisy.

With a new diaper on the baby and a much clearer mind, Becca made her way downstairs to warm a bottle. Not that she was any more eager to come face-to-face with the man she had spent the night with on the sofa, but Daisy was hungry. She found Danny and April at the dining room table with Nick, eating scrambled eggs and toast, and jelly smeared on both Danny and April's faces.

"We've decided to make a snowman," Nick said, matter-of-factly.

Danny bounced in his chair and shouted. "Can we, Mom?"

She shushed him, pointing at Daisy, and then smiled. She hadn't seen her son this excited in months. "If you dress warmly, yes. Hat, gloves, boots, the works."

"Me, too?" April asked.

"You, too."

"Yippee!" they both shouted and scrambled away from the table.

Nick stood, gathering his plate and those that Danny and April had left. "I hope it's okay that I suggested playing in the snow."

"Of course it is," she answered. "Too much time inside, and we'd all be climbing the walls. And you can put down those dishes," she told him as he turned for the kitchen. "I'll get them when I'm finished feeding Daisy."

Nick shook his head. "When I was a kid, we were responsible for our own. Even now, I wouldn't dream of leaving my dishes on the table for somebody else to take care of. I'll be happy to help with the washing, too."

She gave him a dismissive wave. "I'll do those tonight, after the kids are in bed. It doesn't take long."

"The offer still stands."

"Thanks." But she knew she wouldn't take him up on it.

While Danny and April struggled with their snow clothes, Becca fed Daisy and watched Nick helping them. She wasn't short-tempered when it came to her children, but Nick put her to shame with his patience. Their excitement made them extra wiggly.

She tried hard not to think what it would be like to have

Nick around more. Standing at the window, while Daisy tried to crawl across the floor at her feet, she watched the snowball fight going on out in the yard. Danny's cheeks were as red as apples—as were April's—and his eyes glowed with delight. He needed this time to cut loose and play. Jason had never taken the time to get to know his son well, but Nick seemed to enjoy romping outside as much as the kids did, if not more.

But she wondered if this growing relationship between Nick and her children, especially Danny, was wise. Nick was her boss. Granted, they were friends, too, and they had taken the first steps last night to mend the sins of the past. But she didn't expect him to be a substitute daddy. If he tired of the role he was choosing to play now, her children would be crushed. When they moved, that could easily happen, and they didn't deserve to have it happen to them again. They had already lost one dad. She would have to be more careful about relying on Nick.

Outside, they were making progress on the snowman they'd begun after obviously tiring of the snowball fight. While Nick rolled snow on a ball to make a bigger one, April and Danny raced into the house, shouting back and forth to each other as they streaked up the stairs.

"Where are you going with those?" Becca asked when they returned, their hands full of clothing.

"The snow family needs clothes," Danny explained.

Before he could escape out the door, she stopped him. "Let me look." Picking through the pile of clothes in his arms and in April's, she pulled out the items she absolutely could not let them take, leaving them with the oldest rags.

"But Mom—"

"Have fun," she told them, opening the door to scoot them outside. Danny grumbled, but as soon as he saw what Nick was doing, he took off at a run.

Becca took a few minutes to check on Daisy, who needed a diaper change, and picked up the remnants of the scramble for snowman clothes, dumping the odds and ends in a box upstairs. On her way back down with Daisy, a thought struck her.

Snow family?

Watching from the window with Daisy in her arms, her question was answered. Four miniature snow people stood in a line in the front yard, while a fifth, spaced a little farther from the others, was being built. She laughed at the snowlady that represented her, easily recognizable by the battered straw hat that perched on its head. Danny's snowboy sported a pair of earmuffs that she thought had been permanently lost. April's snowgirl seemed to be preening in a small red cowgirl hat.

"Look, Daisy," she said, shifting to point out the window. "See the baby?"

Daisy the snowbaby appeared to be crawling at the base of the snowlady, an old baby bonnet perched on her head as she gazed upward. The sight of it all made happy tears well in Becca's eyes.

And then she saw the new snowman, standing apart from the others. Danny, with Nick's help, placed a hard hat on top of its head, and a pair of very worn work gloves adorned the two skinny sticks that represented his arms. But what stopped her heart was the huge question mark, carved into the middle of the snowman for only her to see. Beside the frozen creation, Nick tickled April and chased after Danny.

She knew it now, and couldn't deny it. She had fallen in love again with Nick, if she had ever fallen out. But this time it was dangerous. She had to put an end to it, before he ever suspected.

Chapter Nine

It was late in the morning when Nick pushed open the door to the job trailer and stepped inside, wondering what to expect. The snow had stopped the day before, but some of the work continued with a skeleton crew. Becca's car was parked with the few others, so he knew she was here. But which "she" would he find?

Ever since he and Becca's kids had come in from building their snow family, she had avoided him. She had been pleasant, cordial and eager to get rid of him. He'd said goodbye to the little ones, while Becca had held her front door open for him, a smile frozen on her lips. For some reason, he was no longer welcome.

"I see you made it here okay," he said, pulling off his coat and gloves. "Did you have any trouble?"

Usually, Becca would look up the second he walked in. Today, one day after what he was beginning to refer to as *The Freeze,* she hesitated to look his way and greet him.

All she did was offer him a cursory glance before going back to whatever it was she was doing. "It wasn't bad," she answered with a shrug.

Usually, she was on her feet, ready to pour him a steaming mug of coffee. Today, she continued to work.

Giving a shrug of his own, he started for the coffee-maker. It didn't make any difference to him who poured it. He was a big boy and could get it himself, and he had never expected Becca to do it.

In a flash, she was on her feet and intercepted him. "I'll get it."

"It's okay," he told her. "I don't mind."

Her answer was a shake of her head as she reached for the carafe.

He took a step back and studied her, almost detecting a tremble in her hand when she reached for his cup next to the coffeemaker. Almost. He couldn't be sure.

When she had the cup filled, he moved to take it from her, but instead of handing it to him the way she *usually* did, today she set it on the edge of her desk and returned to her seat, without a sound or even a smile.

There was only one word for it. Weird.

"Thanks," he said, picking up the mug. Instead of taking that first, steadying sip, he watched her pick up a pen and scribble something on a piece of paper, a frown causing a crease on her forehead.

This wasn't working out too well and not at all the way he had expected. Clearing his throat, he eventually found something she might be willing to say more than two words about. "How are the kids after playing out in the snow yes-terday? Any sign of sniffles?"

"They're fine."

And that was it? Okay, maybe she wasn't having a good morning. It happened. Maybe the drive in through all the snow, even though the snowplows had been over all the roads in the area, had been stressful. Maybe she had other things on her mind.

Like maybe her rent or paying her bills or where she was going to live? He ducked that thought. This wasn't the time to confess his current sins. It could be anything. After all, hadn't he encouraged her to buy Christmas presents with part of her pay? It might have been the wrong thing to do. Becca had always struck him as responsible, and after what she had told him about her father, yeah, he could understand how a lot of things might cause her unnecessary worry. She was *too* responsible. Sometimes she cared too much. And the more she continued to freeze him out, the more he began to wonder why *he* cared.

"I'll be in my office." Turning on his heel without waiting for a reply, he made a beeline for the only place he could go to get away from this strange side of her, without going outside and braving the cold. It was cold enough inside, thanks to her. It was entirely possible that whatever it was that was bothering her was his fault. And that just made him feel worse. He hoped that getting a little work done would take care of that.

But he didn't work. Instead, he thought about the same things that had kept him awake the night before.

Could it be that he had dreamed the conversation by the fire? He had thought things were better between them. If it hadn't been a dream, maybe he had read too much into it. If that was the case, he needed to back up and regroup.

Was it that they had fallen asleep—together—while talking and spent the night—together—on the sofa? But nothing had happened, not even a kiss. He'd made sure of that, even though it hadn't been what his body had wanted.

More than an hour later, when the buzz from the phone intercom had him jerking his head up and his mind to the present, not a bit of work had gotten done.

"Yes?" he asked, hoping to find a more cordial and *normal* Becca on the other end.

"John Stapleton is on line one."

"Thanks." He heard the click disconnecting the intercom and couldn't stop the sigh that started from deep down. Considering her mood, he was surprised she hadn't called him *Mr. Morelli*.

The conversation with John, one of his suppliers, was quick and completed within minutes. At least it hadn't been another problem. This time, delivery would be held up just for a few days, until the majority of the snow had melted. Nick knew the man's offer was done out of special consideration, and it quickly put him in a better frame of mind—one that he hoped would help him deal with Becca's frame of mind a little better.

Her strange mood had to be caused by something he had said or done. If only he could figure out what it was. Had he gone too far? Not said the right things? Was she now uncomfortable around him and wanting to quit? He hadn't thought so, judging by the way she had snuggled close to him on the sofa, before they had both drifted off to sleep.

As he got to his feet, he decided that she must be embarrassed by what had happened. They had been through that before, but that had been in the office, not in the privacy of her home. There was a difference, but considering the way she sometimes reacted, she might be thinking of quitting her job. He wouldn't let that happen. Finding competent office people often took time. He'd been through it before in Denver, until he'd finally found Carol, a woman who knew her way not only around an office, but also around a busy construction crew. Becca had been a natural at both, and the last thing Nick needed right now was to lose her. Once he and the crew were able to get back to full-time work, they'd be focusing on catching up.

He wasn't going to let her leave. She needed him as much as he needed her. They had finally come to terms with the past, and it didn't need to interfere anymore.

Apparently she hadn't heard him leave his office or walk the short and narrow hall to find her sitting at her desk, her elbows propped on the top of it and her face buried in her hands. It looked worse than he'd thought. Was she that unhappy working here? And why?

He was about to return as quietly as possible to his office when her head slowly lifted. Her eyes drifted open, but widened immediately when she noticed him.

"Uh, are you okay?" he asked, a small knot forming in his stomach.

"I—I was…resting my eyes."

It was the most she had said to him all day, and he hoped it was a good sign, no matter how badly she had stumbled through it.

"I'd better get back to work," she said, angling herself in the chair to look at the computer screen.

"No!" He managed to keep from ducking his head and lowered his voice. "No, it's okay. Maybe you need a break." He fought to find something to say. Anything mildly intelligent would do. "Hey, it's getting close to lunchtime. If you want to go ahead and go—uh, leave—uh, you know what I mean…" He realized he was sounding like a complete fool.

She busied herself with some paperwork. "No, it's all right. I'll finish with this first, and then…"

And then what?

The thought had him taking stock of the situation. There were better ways to deal with this.

He decided that, instead of escaping to his office again, he'd stay put. With the snow, there wasn't much for him to do outside. Clint was handling the small crew with the little work they were able to do. If an emergency arose or he was needed for something, someone would let him know. And being in his office gave him too much time to think. What he needed to do was observe. Maybe she would say something to tip him off. Then he could deal with it.

Spying a chair away from her desk, he sat and propped one foot on his other knee, settling in for however long this might take.

He watched.

She sorted papers, put them in files, pulled more out, took pencils out of the drawer and sharpened them, then put them back. She ran figures on the adding machine, and then repeated it, erasing something on a paper, only to write down something else.

He knew she was trying to look busy, and it made him smile.

He knew she was avoiding him, and the urge to smile vanished.

The whole ordeal was crazy, and he was ready to give

up. He wasn't getting anywhere by watching her, except to get angry.

And then she stood to roll a blueprint. But there was a problem. The storage containers for all the prints were stored next to where he was sitting.

Her slight hesitation to move in his direction was a clear indication of her indecision, but it didn't stop her. She even offered him a slight smile—with barely a glance—as she walked his way.

He waited while she placed the rolled-up print in the canister and capped it, then bent down to put it in with the others. He decided he'd had enough. "Do you know what I do when April gets in one of these moods?" he asked as she straightened.

She turned to look at him. "What mood?"

"Whatever mood it is you're in."

She did one of those eye-roll things that women are famous for and moved to return to her desk. All he could think was that she wasn't going to get away with this any longer.

Leaning forward on the chair, he reached out to her with both hands. "I tickle her," he said, placing his hands just above her waist, and proceeded to do just that.

She slapped at his hands as he pulled her closer. "Stop it!"

"I will, as soon as you laugh."

"I won't—" But she did, and he pulled her to his lap, settling back in the chair again. "Nick, don't!" she cried, but her giggles cut her off before she could protest anymore. "You said—" She laughed until she gasped for air, and he moved her across his lap, stilling his hands but keeping hold of her. "You said you'd quit," she reminded him.

This was the Becca he remembered. Her eyes sparkled and her smile was no longer forced. "I did quit," he said, watching for her reaction, waiting for her to replace it with a frown or to give him that business smile he was beginning to know all too well. That would happen as soon as she realized where she was and what was happening.

"Yes," she said, nodding, "you did. But—"

"You're even more ticklish than April is."

"I can't help it. And that was a mean trick."

"Oh, I have more, if you'd like to see them."

"No, I think I'll pass."

His gaze slowly moved from her eyes to her lips, and the need to kiss her was all he could think about. He fought it. And he fought it more as he slowly lowered his head.

She shifted slightly and placed a hand on his shoulder. "Nick," she whispered in a sigh.

Her touch was all it took to vanquish the fight, and he pressed his lips to hers as need replaced reason. When her hand gently slid from his shoulder to the back of his neck, and her other hand rested on his chest, he coaxed her lips to open for him. He slipped his hand beneath the bottom of her sweatshirt and nearly lost all control at the feel of her heated silky skin. Deepening the kiss, he explored the sweetness he had never forgotten, until the sound of voices jerked him out of the moment.

Becca pulled away at the same time he did, and they both shot to their feet as the door opened and his parents walked in.

"I hope we're not interrupting anything," his mother said, looking from him to Becca.

Nick ran a hand through his hair and silently cursed his

parents for their bad timing and himself for his own lack
of control. Beside him, Becca turned her back to them all
as she fumbled with the tubes of blueprints.

"That should be all of them," she said to Nick as she
turned to face them with a smile. "I was just straightening
up before I leave for lunch."

Nick didn't miss her flushed cheeks, and he suspected
his mother didn't, either. "I was just getting ready to go out
and check on the crew," he said.

Becca had slipped around them and to the door, where
she grabbed her coat. "It's always nice to see both of
you," she said and was outside before anyone could
respond.

"Well," his mother said, when silence followed Becca's
retreat, "it looks like everything is good here."

Nick knew by the gleam in her eyes exactly what she
was thinking. But *good* wasn't the word he would've used.
In fact, it might turn out to be exactly the opposite.

"I NEED TO APOLOGIZE FOR... well, for what happened earlier."

Becca didn't know whether to laugh or cry at his apology.
Feeling her face infuse with heat at the memory of the kiss
and how badly she hadn't wanted it to stop, she was glad he
wasn't looking at her. "Me, too," she managed to say.

She had escaped the trailer earlier, when his parents
had arrived at the most inopportune moment, to clear her
head and calm her pounding heart. Lunch at a local ham-
burger place—a splurge given her monetary situation—had
helped. After she had gone over what had led to their kiss,
she had admitted to herself that she had been a willing par-
ticipant. It hadn't been completely Nick's fault.

He looked up to meet her gaze. "You've been acting... funny over the past two days, and I was trying to get you to loosen up."

Becca couldn't keep from laughing. "You certainly did that."

Nick's laughter joined hers. "I guess I did. So can we forget about it?"

She didn't think it was something she would ever forget. When he had put his hands on her waist and pulled her backward, her defenses had vanished, and she had gone willingly. Or as willing as a person caught in a fit of giggles could. She could have fought him, insisted that he let her go, but she hadn't. She was as complicit in the kiss as he was, and maybe even more. She had wanted it since she had awakened in his arms the morning before. And that frightened her.

"I think we're even," she reminded him, thinking of how she had let her own enthusiasm lead her to their other kiss in the office. She thought of it as *The Indiscretion,* when she allowed herself to think of it at all. Unfortunately, she found herself thinking about it quite often.

"As long as you don't shut me out again," he said.

Her mind kept telling her that she should, and even a part of her heart did the same. It wasn't that she wanted to, but she knew she had to.

"We were getting along, weren't we?" he asked when she didn't say anything.

"Yes."

"Then why—"

She reached for the ringing phone, relieved she didn't have to answer what she felt sure Nick was going to ask her. "Big Sky Construction," she answered. Keeping her attention on what the caller was saying, she avoided looking at Nick. When the call was complete, she hung up and turned to him. "The delivery you've been waiting on should be here at any time. The truck is on the way."

Nick walked to the window that looked out on the job site. "I'll have to find Clint and pull some men to help unload." Grabbing his coat and hard hat, he turned back to her. "Call me on the two-way if you need me."

He was out the door before she could assure him she would. She had noticed that he looked worried and wondered if it was about what had happened earlier or simply something with the delivery. Whatever it was, she was certain she'd find out in good time.

Returning to her desk, she found some work to keep her mind busy and did her best to keep her thoughts off of Nick. It wasn't easy. In the midst of adding a column of figures, she would suddenly almost feel Nick's arms around her again. Instead of pushing the feeling aside the way she should have, she lost herself in it, then suddenly she would realize what she was doing and force herself back to the figures in front of her.

But she couldn't deny that she was worried. If Nick asked more questions, she didn't know how she would answer him. She enjoyed her job. She enjoyed working for him, although probably more than she should. But she was afraid she was reading more into his feelings for her than what there really was, and she couldn't risk that.

If only she hadn't realized that she was in love with him and probably always had been. She could deal with what would happen when nothing came of this attraction or whatever it was he might be feeling. But she didn't want her children to be hurt because she couldn't control her heart.

Over an hour passed before Nick returned, and he still wore a look of indecision. Becca wasn't sure what to think when he walked past her on his way to his office and said nothing. It wasn't like Nick to do that.

Halfway down the hall, he stopped and turned back. "Will you have dinner with me tonight?"

Becca stared at him and answered without giving it a thought. "Yes, I'd like that."

NICK WAS ABLE TO GET a corner table for two at one of the upscale restaurants in Wichita. Soft lighting encouraged private, quiet conversation, and the service was proving to be excellent. On a busy Friday night, all of that was practically unheard of. But as he had suspected when he was young and living on the wrong side of the tracks, money talked.

"You aren't worried about the kids, are you?" he asked after the waiter had brought their drinks.

Becca shook her head before taking a sip of her wine. "I know they're in good hands with Raylene."

It had taken some doing to make arrangements, but when Raylene had offered to take Danny, April and Daisy not only for the evening, but for the night, Nick had jumped at the chance. He had picked up Becca at her friend's house and hadn't been able to take his eyes off of her since then. He couldn't remember her ever looking more beautiful, in the simple black dress she wore.

Leaning back in her chair, she looked around the room. "I've never been here. It's nice."

"It's my first time, too. One of our suppliers recommended it." He was pleased to know that it wasn't somewhere her ex-husband had brought her.

As they made small talk about what interesting sites there were in the city and how much it had changed, he compared the girl he once knew to the woman across the table from him. At seventeen, Becca had been pure sweetness, from her smile to the way she moved. She was still the same now, but her sweetness had matured into a womanly loveliness and a generosity that would be hard for any woman to measure up to. She was as classy as ever, but she didn't realize it. He decided to blame that on her ex, and couldn't feel bad that he was glad the guy was out of the picture. He only wished she hadn't had to go through the tough times he knew she had faced recently. That *was* her ex's fault.

"I've always been jealous of you," she told him, gaining his full attention.

"For what?"

She glanced down, and then raised her gaze to his. "Your family."

Nick laughed. If only she knew what a pain his family could be, although he had to admit that most of the time he wouldn't want it any other way. They were the reason he had come back to Katyville. Not just the house, although he would hate to lose it.

"You don't know them, then," he replied. "Growing up without wasn't a lot of fun sometimes. You were the one with the advantages."

"Advantages aren't everything."

"They can help."

"And they can hinder."

Knowing what he knew now, he had to agree. "You're right. Maybe a mix of both is good."

She leaned forward, and the light from the candle seemed to make her face glow. "Heavy on the family though."

He thought back to his childhood. Doing without hadn't hurt any of his brothers and sisters, each of them successful now in his or her own way. "You're right," he said. "Now that I think about it, my family *has* done well, even though we all had to work hard to get where we are."

"There's nothing wrong with hard work. It builds character." She settled back in her chair again, a wistful expression on her face as she twirled the stem of her wine glass. "Sometimes I wonder what it would have been like if my mother had lived."

Reaching across the table, he covered her hand with his. "It was hard for you to lose her."

She nodded and sighed softly. "Things changed after she was gone. My father was always protective, but without Mom to temper it, he was worse. He was lost without her and it made him afraid of losing me, too." Her gaze met his across the table. "Don't blame him for what happened. I did, for a long time, but I've finally come to understand him better."

"If you don't blame him, how can I?" He was surprised at his own forgiveness. After all these years of thinking she was cold and heartless, and her father was even worse, he understood why she had done what she had. His heart wasn't nearly as good as hers. Maybe tonight was the time to tell her about the house.

But before he could form the thoughts that would become words, their waiter appeared with their dinner. They reverted again to small talk, this time about Katyville and how it had changed since they were young.

"Do you like that it's grown?" he asked her.

She shrugged one slender shoulder. "There are pros and cons. I'd prefer if it didn't get too much bigger. I don't want it to lose its charm."

"Then you may be disappointed. The exodus from bigger urban areas to small towns like Katyville won't stop soon," he pointed out. "But I agree. And it has changed."

Or maybe it was that he was seeing it with different eyes than he had when he was young. Being the oldest of six children, he had held a grudge toward those who had more. Age and experience had taught him that he had been wrong to do that, yet he knew his feelings still lingered. He hadn't been especially quiet about it when he was young, and it had probably contributed to Becca's father insisting that she stop seeing him. He knew he had been a good kid— his parents had seen to that—but he'd had his rebellious moments. Those had vanished when he started seeing Becca. Still, he was old enough now to realize that the resentment wasn't all bad—it had been a big part of making him who he was today.

"Whether Katyville continues to grow or not, I'm glad I came back," he told her as they finished their meal. "I'd like it to keep its charm, but still keep up with civic advancements."

Across the table from him, Becca nodded. "I was a member of the planning committee that looked into growth a few years ago. What do you think makes Katyville so charming?"

"Just being a small community, I guess. I've never given it much thought. Maybe the fact that everyone pretty much knows everybody else?"

"That's part of it," she agreed. She tilted her head to the side and studied him. "You were going to be an architect."

He smiled, thinking of the past, but knew he needed to be careful about what he said. "I went to college to become one, and did, but I wanted something more hands-on. I was lucky that not long after I started my first job in construction, I found a partner, and we started our own company." He didn't mention that his partner had been the father of the woman he married. "He agreed to let me buy him out two years ago."

"I remember," she said, a faraway look in her eyes. "You wanted to go into restoration, taking old houses and—"

She ducked her head and his heart pounded. The old Watkins place was going to be *theirs*. Was that why it had become so important to him to own it? Because it had been not only his dream, but also hers? He couldn't say it was, but he couldn't say it wasn't, especially when he had been ready to tear it down when he learned she was living in the house that was to have been theirs.

When she finally lifted her head and looked at him, the faraway look was gone and she was smiling. "It's funny how things change."

Words stuck in his throat, so he agreed with a nod. Would she guess now that he had bought the house? That he was the one who was forcing her to leave it? He knew this could be the right time to bring that up, yet he couldn't. It would take finding the right words and, at the moment, he couldn't even speak. By telling her, the evening might be ruined, and so would the tenuous friendship they'd been building. Did he want to risk that right now?

"But you're building new ones instead," she continued, as if the stroll through the past had never happened.

Relief flooded through him. He would save the confession for later. "Give me time," he told her with a conspiratorial wink that he instantly regretted.

"Will the crew be able to do that?"

Now he was on solid ground. This he could talk about, without guilt eating away at him. "Most will. We have a good crew. Those who don't have the skills for restoration can be taught. It'll take time though. And speaking of the crew…"

"They're a great group. I'd like to get to know them—and their families—better."

He was pleased to hear it. "Then the proposition I'm about to offer you will give you the chance to do that."

"Proposition?" she asked.

He nodded, eager to present it to her and hoping she would accept. It had been one of the reasons he had asked her to dinner, along with being able to spend time alone with her, without kids, business, family and everything else that never ceased to interrupt.

"In the past," he continued, "we've had a party each year at Christmastime. It's always been catered, and sometimes we've even had a gift exchange. Families are encouraged to attend, and I always manage to find the perfect Santa to pass out a small gift to each child."

"Nick, that's wonderful!" Her eyes sparkled as she leaned forward. "Tell me more."

He gave her a slow grin. "I'd like you to be the hostess this year."

Her eyes widened and she sank back against her chair. "Me?"

"You'd be perfect," he told her sincerely. "You're familiar with nearly every member of the crew, and you probably even know their wives' names and how many kids they have." When her brows furrowed, he hurried on. "There won't be that much work to it. I already have the Santa, know who'll be doing the catering and what will be served and the gifts are being taken care of. Your job would be to make everyone feel welcome. And I know you can do that without even trying. So what do you say? Will you do it?"

She hesitated for a moment, and finally smiled. "Yes, of course I will. I'll need more details though."

BECCA COULDN'T PUT a name to the way she felt as Nick explained what she would be doing for the Christmas party, but disappointment gnawed quietly at her heart.

Was this why he had asked her to dinner tonight? Oh, sure, they had talked about personal things, but hadn't she initiated a lot of that? And here she had thought— She gave a silent sigh. How foolish it had been of her to think this dinner was a *date*.

It wasn't that she wasn't flattered to be asked to play hostess. If fact, she looked forward to getting to know the crew and their families better. And it seemed that most of the planning had already been done, so there wasn't a lot for her to do, except make certain everything was in order and to make the event enjoyable. Nothing she couldn't handle, even on a bad day.

But it still hurt to realize that Nick had invited her to dinner to spring this on her. She wished she hadn't let her imagination, not to mention her heart, run away with her. But at least she had caught her slip about the house. At least he still didn't remember about the plans they'd made so long ago. There was no telling what he might think, if and when he did.

Next time, she would know better than to think that he shared her feelings and memories about— She was too disappointed in herself to even finish the thought.

Chapter Ten

With the snow from the previous week completely gone and much of the melting dried, the slowdown in construction was a thing of the past. Becca kept busier than ever in the office and was thankful for it. She had spent the night after her dinner with Nick at Raylene's, and on Saturday they had gone shopping for a new dress for the company Christmas party. After paying bills and the rent owed, she still had enough money to buy a dress on sale. With only a week until Christmas Eve, everything was a flurry of activity. It was exciting. It was nerve-wracking. It helped her keep her mind off of her personal life.

Because it was payday, men were in and out of the trailer, one or two at a time, throughout the afternoon. Over the weekend, she had taken the initiative to make Christmas cards with reminders about the party for each of the crew, and as they came in for their checks, she made sure each one received one. Because Christmas would come early during the next workweek, Nick had given everyone extra time off with pay, as a Christmas bonus. This week would end on Wednesday, and she wanted to make sure everyone was aware of the time and date of the party. She couldn't help but be excited.

"You'll be at the party on Saturday, won't you?" she asked Clint, Nick's foreman, as she handed him his pay-check and the card.

He took it from her and flashed a grin. "Wouldn't miss it for the world. The boss says you'll be runnin' the show, and the missus is looking forward to meeting you."

"I'm eager to meet her, too," Becca replied, "and all of the wives and families. I just hope everything goes smoothly."

Giving her a fatherly pat on the shoulder, he laughed. "You'll do fine. Just being together is the best part of it. And the boss is always generous, so no matter what happens, it's a great time for everybody. Don't recall any that weren't, and I've been around for a long time."

Becca leaned against the edge of her desk. "You've known Nick for several years, haven't you?"

"Ever since he started Big Sky. That'd be almost seven years now. Best boss I've ever had, and let me tell you, I've had a few."

"He has impressed me, too," she admitted.

"Fresh out of college, he was, with all kinds of big ideas. Funny thing was those ideas worked for him, when they wouldn't have worked for a lot of other people." He glanced down and hesitated, then looked up again. "It's probably none of my business, but you and the boss go back a ways, don't you?"

Becca felt the faint heat of a blush and willed it away, hoping she could find an acceptable explanation of their past relationship, without saying too much. "Back when I was in high school, mostly. He left for college before I graduated. It was a surprise to learn he'd come back to Katyville."

"Yup. But he never seemed to act like he was comfortable back in Denver." Clint leaned down, a conspiratorial gleam in his eye. "Now don't you tell him I told you that."

"I won't."

Straightening, he continued. "He seems a lot happier here. You know, I've lived all over this great country, at one time or another, and I can honestly say that this is a good place to live. The missus and I like it here."

Before Becca could answer, Nick walked in. Clint thanked her, greeted Nick and bid her goodbye, leaving her alone with Nick.

"Did you make up these cards?" Nick asked her, picking up one from her desk and reading it.

Becca bit her lip, afraid she had done something she shouldn't have. "Yes, I did. I hope it's all right."

He looked directly at her. "All right? Hey, it's great! I knew you'd put your special touch on this party."

She should have been bursting with pride, but her happiness was dimmed by the fact that, in spite of the night of the snowstorm, she was now certain their dinner had been for business purposes only, not because he was interested in her. She regretted making any of it personal and bringing up the past. It was now clear to her that he cared for her as only a friend would, kiss notwithstanding, and she would be better off if she would accept that.

"Thank you," she managed to say.

"Are Danny and April excited about the party?"

She nodded. "Getting to see Santa is all they could talk about last night. I was wishing I had waited to tell them."

He stepped back to lean against the outside door and crossed his arms on his broad chest. "My ex-wife didn't want kids. I wish I'd known that before I slipped the ring on her finger. I've always wanted a family."

"I'm sorry, Nick," she said, not knowing what else she could say.

His sudden smile touched her heart. "Your kids are the greatest," he said. "I have to admit I'm crazy about them. I mean, my nieces and nephews are great, too, but they're family. I appreciate you letting me get to know Danny and April and Daisy."

Everything began to come together for her, and it took all her strength not to let him see that his comment hurt. Her kids were the reason he had been so kind. From the very beginning, he'd paid attention to them, teased them, talked to them. His confession was proof of her suspicion that she was nothing more than a friend—a fringe benefit with kids and made easier because they had known each other in the past. It wasn't her that he really cared about, it was her children.

With an effort, she willed back the tears that threatened. "They like you, too," she forced herself to say.

He took a step away from the door and was rewarded by it flying open to slam into him.

His parents walked in, and his mother frowned at him. "Nicky, don't stand by the door."

Nick rubbed at the back of his head where the door had hit him, a wry grin on his face. "Yes, ma'am. What brings you two back again?" He glanced at his father, standing behind his mother.

Elena walked over to Becca and gave her a quick hug. "We wanted to remind you that we'll be wrapping the children's gifts for the party on Wednesday night," she said

to Nick. "And we wanted to invite Becca to join us for it."
She gave him a strange look that Becca couldn't decipher.

"Whatever Becca wants to do," Nick answered with a
shrug.

She looked from him to his mother, and even glanced at
his father, who surprised her by winking at her. In spite of
her revelation about Nick, his family would always be special
to her, and she smiled back at him. "It sounds like fun."

"You'll need to find a babysitter," Elena was telling her,
"because we'll be wrapping gifts from Santa, you see. Will
that be trouble for you?"

Becca shook her head, knowing Raylene would gladly
take the kids for the evening, especially if it had anything
to do with Nick or his family. "I'm sure I can find someone."

"Good." Elena took the chair Nick moved closer to her,
and her husband went to stand next to her, nodding with a
smile at Becca. "It isn't that I don't want to see them again,"
Elena explained. "They are beautiful *bambinos,* Becca,
and so smart."

"Thank you," she said. She was pleased that Elena
thought so much of her children.

Elena reached out to take her hand. "You are doing a fine
job with them, *cara.* Being a mother alone is difficult, but
they are wonderful children. Nicky mentioned the same
thing to me after he watched after them for Gabrielle."

Nick had watched her children? Becca glared at him.
They'd discuss this when his parents were gone. "They're
very fond of him, too," she told his mother.

Elena released her, but not without an extra loving squeeze.
"They enjoyed the snow family? I wanted to ask you when
we were here last, but you were going off to lunch."

Becca knew the reminder of that day had caused her cheeks to redden. "Yes, but they're all melted now."

"There'll be more snow. More snow families. And other things."

Becca wondered if she could feel any more embarrassed than she did at that moment. Thankfully, Nick came to her rescue.

"Mama," he said, helping her from her chair, "we have business to do here. You'll see Becca Wednesday night and can talk about the snow then."

She patted his cheek. "You're a good boy, Nicky. Of course, you have work to do. We won't bother you more today." Turning to Becca she said, "Don't forget. Wednesday evening. Six-thirty. And bring your appetite."

Becca assured her she would be there and avoided looking directly at Nick.

Elena started out the door, but turned back. "I forgot. It's Tony's birthday, too. So we'll be having a— What do you call it? Two-er?"

"Twofer," Nick said.

"That's it," Elena said, and turned to Becca. "But you've already been invited, correct?"

"Yes, thank you. I'll be there, too." Not that she had planned to be, but she considered it part of her job to help with the Christmas party gifts, and to decline the party would be rude.

When Nick's parents had gone, Becca spun around to face him, her temper at the point of boiling. First her discovery of how he really saw her, and now this. "And just when was it that you watched my kids? And when were you going to tell me about it?"

NICK'S MOUTH HAD gone dry the moment his mother mentioned that he had covered for Gabby, and now it took an effort to swallow before answering Becca. "The day it snowed, while you were picking up the blueprints. I was going to tell you—"

She took a step toward him, her hands on her hips and her eyes flashing fury. "You had all that evening, that night, and half of the next day, not to mention our dinner and at anytime here in the office, yet you never mentioned it. Why not?"

He had only one answer. The truth. "I forgot. And I was only there for—"

"It doesn't matter how long it was," she said, her voice nearing a growl. "What matters is that no one—*no one*—thought to tell me about this. Not even Gabby." She walked around her desk and sat down hard on her chair.

Nick took a deep breath, planted his palms on the top of her desk and leaned over it. "If you remember, we were in a rush when we picked them up at Gabby's. There was barely time to get them bundled up and out the door, let alone talk about the day."

She refused to look at him, and crossed her arms. "She could have told me the next day."

"She didn't see you the next day," he reminded her, keeping his voice low and even, so as not to rile her again. "I was snowed in at your house, and I'm sure she was busy dealing with her own family." He paused to let that sink in. "Including her mother-in-law."

Becca glanced at him, a wariness in her eyes. "Her mother-in-law lives on the outskirts of town."

"Yes," he said, nodding, "and Gabby needed to take a prescription out to her that day, before the roads got so bad that she couldn't. She had five kids there, Becca. She needed to hurry. *You* know how long it takes to get coats and gloves on *three* and get them in the car."

But Becca wasn't buying it. "Explanations are irrelevant at this point. What matters is that my children were left with you, without my knowledge."

"She asked for you when she called, but considering the weather that day, I wouldn't have allowed you to go anyway." He paused to take a deep breath. "They were in good hands, Becca. Surely you know that."

"And just what do *you* know about children?"

Nick stared at her, completely baffled that she could say that. "What do I know? I was the oldest of six, Becca. I think I have at least a clue."

Her face took on a pink shade as she ducked her head. "I'd forgotten."

He suddenly understood. This lioness was protecting her children. But he wondered why she felt they needed to be protected from him?

"We all forget, now and then," he pointed out. "Even you."

"Of course," she said. "I'm sor—"

"No, don't say it. Don't say you're sorry. You have every right to be angry. I should've told you."

"I shouldn't have yelled at you."

"I wasn't aware that you had such a hot temper," he told her with a grin.

Her answering smile was on the watery side.

He pulled his hands from her desk and straightened. "If Gabby had known it would upset you so much, I'm sure she would have arranged something else. She called you here, first. Because there wasn't time to wait for you to get back from the city, I was happy to lend a hand. After all, two of those kids are my niece and nephew."

Becca nodded, but still didn't look at him. "I trust you with mine, too. I know you wouldn't let anything happen to them."

He wasn't sure what to think, except that she was only being protective. But he couldn't understand why she should feel she needed to protect them from him.

She looked tired, as if she'd been fighting a major battle. And maybe she had. In an effort to make things easier for her, he might have made them worse for both of them. Maybe hiring her had been the wrong thing to do, but he wasn't willing to let her go.

A glance at his watch told him that it was nearing the end of the day. "Why don't you go on home?" he suggested. "I can pass out the rest of the checks—and those cards, too—although I'm sure they'd rather see your pretty smile than me when they pick them up."

His offer was apparently enough to allow her to look at him. "Would you mind?" she asked. "I'll come in early to make up the time."

"No need to do that. I'd rather you got some rest tonight and come in at the same time." When she started to argue, he put his hand up. "Consider it paid time off."

"I don't deserve it, but—" She pushed to her feet, looking almost weary. "Thanks. I think I will go home."

He waited while she gathered her things, and then made sure she made it to her car and had driven away before he took a seat behind her desk. Breathing out a long sigh, he leaned back and stared at the ceiling of the tiny trailer. But it wasn't the water spots on the ceiling tiles he was looking at. It was Becca's smile and the love he always saw in her eyes for her children.

He thought about his mother's invitation to Becca to join them for the wrapping party. *Still matchmaking, Mama?* He smiled, knowing she was and also knowing it was out of love for him. And for Becca, too.

He was all for Becca being a part of the party, but he wasn't so sure it was a good idea for her to be around them. His mother was infamous for saying what might be better left unsaid, and he knew she was suspicious enough about his feelings for Becca. What else might she pick up on?

He hadn't been surprised when Becca had accepted the invitation, especially knowing how she felt about his family. He hoped her opinion wouldn't change after spending an evening with them. They were loud. They were boisterous. And they loved each other. Maybe she could overlook the first two.

He was certain about only one thing. He didn't want to lose her. The more he thought about that, the more he began to realize that it wasn't her secretarial skills that he would miss if she left. Nor was it that he would miss the bond he had formed with her kids.

He would miss *her.* Becca. Not the young girl he had loved ten years earlier, but the woman she had become.

Had he ever *stopped* loving her? And because he knew it, he had to tell her the truth about the house. As soon as the company party was over on Saturday, he would tell her. He only hoped she would understand. But even if it took years for her to forgive him, he had to come clean, before things went any further.

BECCA STOOD ON the Morellis' porch, shivering. But it wasn't the cold that made her body shake in short spasms. It was nerves. She had known the family since she was a little girl. She had even been to their home once, when she and Nick were dating and he needed to pick up something he'd forgotten. They had always been warm and accepting of her—something her father had never been toward them. A small amount of tolerance toward others was all he had ever had.

Glancing at her watch, she realized that if she hesitated much longer about ringing the doorbell, she'd be considered late. Even her mother would have frowned on that.

As her gloved finger neared the button, she wondered again why she had accepted Elena Morelli's invitation to join them. But it had been Elena issuing it, and Becca wouldn't have known how to turn her down. In truth, she had always thought the world of Nick's mother.

Taking a deep, steadying breath, she rang the bell and instantly heard voices shouting inside the house.

"Get the door, Nicky," she heard Elena call out over the other voices.

A few seconds later, the door opened to reveal a grinning Nick. "I see you didn't chicken out."

Becca gathered every single ounce of courage that she could. His grin helped. "Me? Chicken out? Surely you jest, sir."

He opened the door wider and waved her inside. "Then welcome to the Morelli Madhouse. Check your mind at the door."

Becca laughed, relaxing, and stepped inside a wide hallway, where a gorgeous old staircase led up to her right. A jewel-toned rug lay beneath her feet.

"It's as beautiful as I remember it," she told him.

"You remember it? You were only here once that I know of."

She flashed him a smile of superiority. "Once was all I needed."

"Nicky, bring her in here with the rest us," his mother said, her voice floating from behind doors to their left. "Don't be keeping her all to yourself."

Nick groaned and leaned down to whisper in Becca's ear, sending a warm shiver through her. "Are you sure you can handle this?" he asked. "They can get pretty wild. I can help you escape now, before it's too late."

She gave him a playful push. "You forget that I've been here in Katyville all the time you were off at college and building your company. I know most of them better than I know you."

His hot, piercing gaze set off a spark of fire deep within her. "Are you sure about that?"

Breathless from the rush going through her body and wishing she could stop it, she nodded.

"Nick!"

He cringed at his mother's reminder.

"Come on, Nick. Share," someone else could be heard saying.

There was laughter and teasing coming from the room behind the doors, and she longed to join in.

He draped an arm around her shoulders. "Ready?"

"You're the one holding this up," she pointed out.

Leading her through the set of double doors, he stepped into the room, where his family waited with welcoming smiles. "You know everybody then?" he asked her.

She nodded as Gabby greeted her. "Come sit by me, Becca."

"Greedy," Gabby's sister, Ann-Marie, said and stuck out her tongue. "You see her almost every day."

Gino, who was the second oldest, patted the space next to him. "Sit here, Becca," he called to her, while his wife, Karen, on the other side of him nodded in agreement. "You'd be wise to stay out of the middle of their catfight."

"Gino!" Elena warned from a doorway, but her angry tone didn't hide her laughing eyes.

Without a word, Nick led her to an empty place across from Tony and his wife, Beth. "Feeling a little overwhelmed now?" Nick whispered as he settled beside her.

"Only a little." She handed the package she'd brought to Tony and was pleased with his surprised thanks. Looking around the room at the family members, she noticed one missing. "Is Angelo still in St. Louis?"

Elena nodded. "He and Janine will be here this weekend with their little ones and plan to stay at least a week."

Becca counted heads. With spouses and Ann-Marie's fiancé, there were an even dozen, including herself, in the room. She could only imagine what it was like when all the children and babies were there, too.

"Come, come," Elena urged them. "It's time to eat."

"Typical," Nick grumbled quietly beside her. "As soon as you sit down, she's ready to feed you."

Becca gave him a long, slow, head-to-toe inspection, appreciating every inch of him and not ashamed to do it. "It doesn't seem to have hurt you." She stood as everyone else did, and watched them. "Nor any of them, either. You couldn't ask for a healthier, happier family."

"It's a good thing I'm not a desk jockey," he told her, "or you wouldn't have that gleam in your eye. You'd be leading me *out* of the dining room instead of *into* it."

She glanced at Carmine Morelli as he took his place at the head of the table. "Your father looks fit."

"He took up golf," Nick whispered as he pulled out a chair for her.

"I should introduce him to my father. Maybe your father could give him a run for his money."

Nick chuckled, taking his place next to her. "He just might, at that."

Dinner was a delight in the overly large dining room that contained a table that held everyone with room to spare. Becca didn't think she had ever seen so much food or so many people enjoying it so much. From ricotta mixed with herbs to beef carpaccio, complete with salad and fruit, the meal was topped off with a heavenly dessert of chocolate-orange biscotti, which she learned was Tony's favorite.

"I'll never eat again," she groaned as Nick helped her from her chair at the end of the meal. "Do you always feast like this?"

"Only when we're all together, although when it's only Mama and Pop and me, we don't do too badly. Someone is always stopping by, so Mama stays prepared."

Becca remembered lonely dinners in her room when her parents were gone to a party or special occasion, or even out for an evening with friends. Even when they were home, meals were often silent and stiff. That's the way her father had liked it, but she had often thought that if there were more kids in her family, it would be different. She had wished, many times, for a brother or sister, but none had ever arrived to keep her company. After she and Raylene had become close, she spent more mealtimes with her friend's family than with her own.

"You really don't know how lucky you are, do you, Nick?" she asked as they returned to the living room and reclaimed their seats.

"Yes, I do. I really do."

A quick glance at him assured her he was serious. And maybe he did know, having been away from them for ten years.

"Who has the list?" Gabby called out.

"I do," Karen answered. "And Ann-Marie brought the gift bags."

Beth sank to the sofa beside her husband and pulled out a paper bag. "Scissors and ribbon, here," she announced and passed around the bag. "Gift tags, too. Don't forget them."

Carmine was the last to join the family, taking the well-worn easy chair not far from where Becca and Nick sat. "How many this year?"

"Forty-one," Tony announced.

Becca turned to Nick. "*This* year?"

He nodded. "They've done this every year since I started the company. They choose the gifts by the age and sex of each child from a list, buy them, get together to wrap them, then ship them off to me."

"That's absolutely amazing," she said in complete awe. "They'll all be at the party, right?"

"Yes. This year they'll get to see how excited the kids are with the gifts."

"Nick," Gino called to him, "come look at this."

"Be right back," Nick told her. "And don't let anybody take my seat."

Beside her in his chair, Carmine leaned closer. "It's good you've come. Nico deserves his own joy."

Before she could think of a way to thank him, he had turned to talk to Elena, and her eyes misted with tears at the feeling of belonging she felt with this family. If only...

"Hey, Nick," Tony said from across the room, "how did your house weather the snowstorm?"

Becca looked up to see Nick standing perfectly still, his eyes widened in horror. "What house?" she asked. "I didn't know you had a house, Nick. Here in Katyville?"

Nick shot Tony a killer glare, but Tony was looking at Becca. "Why, the one you live—" He jammed his jaws together and shook his head.

A cold chill swept through Becca. Slowly, she turned to look at the stunned and suddenly pale man watching her. "Nick?"

The answer to her question was in his eyes.

Chapter Eleven

One look at Becca, and Nick knew it was all over between them. The laughter was gone from her eyes, and the color had drained from her face. Any dreams he might have had of a future with her were gone. It would take a miracle to fix this, and he figured he had run his quota on those.

"What's this?" his mother asked. She looked from Nick to Tony and back again. "What house? You have a house?"

Tony shook his head. "Forget it, Mama. I was…confused. Didn't know what I was talking about."

Her eyes narrowed as she studied her youngest son. "You were never good at covering up, Antonio. Or lying."

"I'll explain later, Mama," Nick said. He had been ready to beat the living daylights out of his youngest brother, but he knew, deep down, that he was the one at fault. He was the one who hadn't been truthful. And he was the one who would pay for that.

To his relief, most of his family had been too busy to notice what was going on. Across the room, Becca was tying a bow on a gift sack, as if she hadn't just been betrayed. He watched as Beth walked over and lowered herself to sit beside her, placing a loving hand on her arm.

Becca shook her head and even managed a smile. Bless Beth, Nick thought. Tony had probably told her the whole story, and both of them had come to the agreement that big brother Nick was the lowest of the low. They weren't far off. He'd never felt this miserable.

Unable to watch and listen to his family's enjoyment of the evening any longer, he escaped to the kitchen. His hands shook as he reached for a glass in the cabinet and filled it with water. He was tempted to add a liberal splash of bourbon, knowing the bottle was within easy reach. This seemed the perfect time to get roaring drunk. Maybe it would blur the memory of the look on Becca's face. But he knew that wouldn't help. He needed to keep his mind sharp, in case he had the chance to talk to her. He drank the glass of water instead.

Tony came into the kitchen, looking almost as miserable as Nick felt. "I don't know what to say, except I've always had a big mouth."

Nick shook his head. "It's my fault, not yours."

"Is there anything I can do?"

The word *no* lodged in Nick's throat, so he shook his head again.

Tony reached for his own glass. As he stuck it under the faucet and filled it, Nick noticed that his brother wasn't all that steady, either.

"I guess I thought you'd told her," Tony said, keeping his voice low.

"No. I couldn't find the right time. Not telling her to begin with only made it worse to own up to it."

Tony nodded his agreement. "Think you can fix it?"

"I—" Nick raked a hand through his hair. "I don't know.

I'd half expected her to walk over and punch me. She has every right. But knowing her, she'll wait until later, when nobody's around, to unleash her well-founded fury."

"Hell hath no fury?" Tony asked with a wry smile.

"Like a scorned woman," their mother finished, walking into the room. Nick didn't correct her as she shooed her sons out onto the sunporch off the kitchen. Placing her hands on her hips, she looked from one of her sons to the other. "You will both tell me what is going on."

Nick didn't think he could handle both his mother's and Becca's scorn in one day, and he knew the latter was coming. He just didn't know when. He looked at Tony, who shrugged.

Dragging up a deep breath, Nick decided he might as well confess. It would be easier now than later, and something he should have done in the beginning. If he was lucky—and he wasn't counting on it—his mother might offer him some of her wisdom, along with the tongue-lashing he expected.

After taking another deep breath, he began. "A few months back, I bought the old Watkins place."

"The house where Becca lives?"

He nodded. "I didn't know she was living there. In fact, I didn't know who was living there, until I found her miles from town with a flat tire in the middle of the night."

His mother stepped closer to him. "But you told her you were the owner of the house."

The air went out of him, and he avoided looking at her, knowing what was coming. "No."

"Oh, Nicky."

Her disappointment was clear in her voice, but Nick wasn't up to defending himself. How could he, when he was so clearly in the wrong?

"She's still paying rent?" his mother asked. When he nodded, she shook her head and *tsk-tsked.* "You're paying her wages only to take them for rent? You know she can't have that much money. What kind of man are you?"

Nicky wasn't sure how to answer. At the moment, he felt like the biggest jerk in the world. "A very sad one, Mama."

She laid her head on his arm and patted him, before stepping back to study him. "You have to fix this, Nicky."

"I know, Mama." But how?

When she was gone, Tony gave him a brotherly pat on the back. "If there's anything I can do…" He stepped away, a sad look on his face. "I know, I've done enough already."

"It's okay," Nick assured him. "I got myself into this. I'll find a way to make it better." He hoped.

He followed Tony back to the living room and discovered that Becca was wearing her coat and was ready to leave. Catching up with her as she stepped into the foyer, he took her elbow. "I'll walk you out to your car."

She gently pulled away. "There's no need. I'm fine."

Her voice was shaky but quiet and not at all what he expected. Maybe it wasn't as bad as he had thought, but he wasn't about to be put off. He might not have any idea of what he should say to her, but he wouldn't let her get away until he could explain.

And beg her forgiveness.

Pulling the door open, he let her pass through ahead of him.

She stepped outside onto the porch and continued to walk toward the steps that would take her down and away from him.

"Becca?"

Stopping, she turned back to look at him. "I want you

to know that the only reason I didn't get up and leave was because of your family, not because of you."

She turned again, moving on, but he caught up with her and put his hand on her arm to stop her. When she glanced back at him, her eyes were blank, with no emotion in their green depths. Letting out the breath he was holding, he closed his eyes to steady himself. He had expected to see hate there. He deserved that. But it dawned on him that she wasn't the type of person who would feel that emotion. She had always been a much better person than he was.

"We need to talk," he said, hoping she'd be willing to listen.

She sighed and closed her eyes. "The time for talking is over, Nick," she said, opening them. "I'll be out of the house by the original date."

"You don't have to do that. You don't have to leave at all. Please."

She continued as if she hadn't heard him. "I'd appreciate it if you would give me a letter of recommendation for a new job. You know my address, so just put it in the mail."

When she turned to leave, his heart hit his throat. "Wait, Becca," he called to her as she stepped down onto the steps. She kept walking, and the darkness surrounded her until he could no longer see where she was. He heard her car door close and her engine engage, and looked in that direction. If he ran, he might catch her before she drove away, but he knew it wouldn't do any good.

The ache in his chest grew heavier, as he watched her drive away, past the house. He'd been through this all before, but this time it hurt more.

This time *he* was to blame.

He stood in the dark until a cold shiver shook him, reminding him that it was winter, not the spring that kept playing through his mind. Wasn't there something he could do? He doubted it. Becca had always had her share of pride, no matter how bad things were for her. Still, as soon as he learned she was his tenant, he had instructed his attorney not to cash the rent checks and to send the rest to him. He hadn't cashed the check for the rent that had arrived that morning. He would tear it up and send her the pieces. He had never planned to take her money.

There were other things he could do. One was to act on a suggestion she had made about his business. Tomorrow he would make some phone calls and see if he could get it rolling. Even if he never saw her again, he would know that he had done something worthwhile that she would approve of, even if she never again approved of him.

"Nick?"

He turned to see Gabby in the doorway, lit by the lights from inside. "She's gone," he said, barely able to speak the words.

He felt her step up behind him and put her arms around him. "Give her some time. She's hurting."

He nodded, wondering just how much time it would take for Becca to be willing to listen to him and maybe forgive him.

Too much, he thought. *If ever.*

"ARE YOU SURE this is what you want to do?"

Becca placed the glass wrapped in newspaper into a box and began wrapping another, not at all willing to go over this yet one more time with her best friend. Raylene was supposed to be helping her pack, not helping her feel worse.

"It's not what I *want* to do," she explained again. "It's what I have to do."

"Did you give him a chance to tell his side of the story?"

"He had plenty of time to do that before Tony slipped up."

"I'm sure he had a reason—"

"Right," Becca said, turning away from her best friend. "Probably the same reason he had for not telling me that he had watched my kids that day. He forgot." She shook her head and went back to packing. "It won't work this time, Raylene."

"You've always been more forgiving of others than of yourself," Raylene said, her voice edged with recrimination. "Try forgiving yourself."

On her knees by the box, Becca nearly dropped the glass in her hand and turned to stare at her friend. "Forgive myself for what?"

Raylene's face softened. "For beating yourself up for ten years. For thinking Nick hated you."

"He did. He admitted it."

"And you think that's why he didn't tell you about this house?"

Becca lifted her shoulder in a shrug, her hands holding tightly to the glass she was wrapping. She didn't know why Nick hadn't told her. She hadn't felt like giving him the opportunity to hurt her even more. "What difference would that make? He knew from that first night that I was his renter, but he didn't bother to tell me. He didn't even hint at it."

"He did give you an extension," Raylene pointed out. "Shouldn't that count for something?"

Becca looked up to see Raylene watching her. "Why? So he could collect another month's rent?"

"He gave you a job, Bec. A way to feed your kids and

pay your bills. He helped make you feel like you were worth something. Even I haven't been able to do that." She shook her head and walked away. "Jason really did a number on you."

"Jason has nothing to do with this."

Raylene sat on the sofa and stretched her arms along the back of it. "You're angry."

"Yes, I am, dammit!" Becca bit her lip and glanced toward the stairway. Swearing was something she rarely did, but of course she was angry. It was the only way to keep from hurting.

"How are the kids taking this?" Raylene asked.

Becca sat back on her heels. "They're okay. Danny asked if Nick was moving with us." Her eyes suddenly filled with tears, and she had to wipe them away with her shirtsleeve. "I reminded him that Nick didn't live with us, and he wanted to know if Nick would come visit us after we've moved."

"And you told him what?"

Thinking back to the conversation she'd had yesterday morning with her son, Becca wanted to let go and cry. But she couldn't. She had made her decision, and she knew it was the best thing for her kids. As far as she was concerned, Danny and April would be better off if they never saw Nick again. In time, they'd forget about him. And maybe she would, too.

She took a deep breath, hoping she could get through it all without breaking down. "I explained that Nick was a friend, but that we'd have lots and lots of new friends."

"He accepted that?"

"He didn't have a choice."

"He adores Nick."

"Which is exactly what I was afraid would happen."

"Becca, it isn't wrong for Danny to care about the man who took the time to pay attention to him and make him happy."

Pressing the heels of her hands to her eyes, Becca shook her head. "I know that, but I also knew that there was a strong possibility that it wouldn't last." She lifted her head and looked across the room at Raylene. "Nick was bound to move on at some point. I think he reveled in Danny's adoration. It made him feel like…"

"A father?" Raylene finished.

Reaching behind her, Becca picked up another glass and began wrapping the newspaper around it. "Maybe. In his own way. I think it was the kids that attracted him. It wasn't me. You saw him that first night when he brought me to your house. He certainly wasn't cheered at the sight of me, much less having to help me." When Raylene opened her mouth to speak, Becca hurried on. "We've been working out the problems we had when we were young, and that's good. At least he now knows the truth about that."

Raylene was quiet for a moment. "Interesting."

Becca looked up. "What is?"

"Oh, only that you were the one who wasn't completely truthful back then, and now you aren't willing to let him explain his transgressions."

"It isn't the same," Becca said, shaking her head.

"Isn't it? Knowing Nick, I'm sure he had good reasons for not telling you he owned this house." She got to her feet and left the room, heading into the kitchen.

Becca stopped wrapping. Raylene might have a point. Becca knew Nick was a good man. He always had been.

But nothing had ever been right between them. Honesty had always been a problem. She had deceived her father by sneaking out to see Nick, and then she had coldly dumped him, never telling him the truth about why. Not to mention that now that they were working on slaying those old ghosts, they had been constantly apologizing to each other for their attraction to each other, first her and then him. It was only natural they might still have some old feelings left over. If he loved her kids as much as she suspected he did, it was only natural that he tried to make her happy, too. Besides that, she was certain he didn't want to lose a good secretary and be forced to train a replacement.

Raylene returned and handed her a mug of hot tea. "What about the company party?"

Becca had asked herself the same question, and decided that she couldn't go. As much as she loved Nick, she was afraid she might be fool enough to accept an apology from him. That would only be a disaster. Things were better left as they were—for everybody.

"I'm not going," she answered.

"Scared?"

"A little," she admitted.

"Everyone will miss you."

"And I'll miss seeing them and meeting their families and seeing the joy on the faces of the children when Santa visits. But it would be a bad idea."

"Would it help if I went with you?"

Becca considered it, but knew it wouldn't change anything. "It might, but what for?"

"You really should go, if for no other reason than to tell the crew goodbye."

"I know, and I'll think about it," Becca said. "But that's all. No promises that I'll go."

"GREAT PARTY, Mr. Morelli."

Nick did his best to smile through the friendly slap on the back and wished this whole ordeal would be over with soon. Every one of his employees was here—except one— and asking where Becca was. He had hoped earlier, when the party began, that she would show up, but as time wore on, he realized he had been a fool to even think she would consider it.

Gabby walked up to him with little Cat in her arms. "I know," he told her, forcing a smile. "Give her time."

When his niece reached out to him, he took her and held her close. She placed her soft cheek on his and sighed. "Nickeee," she whispered. He hugged her even closer.

Gabby looked around at the crowd, and then quickly turned back to him, concern in her eyes. "She's here, Nick. She just walked in."

He craned his neck to see the door and saw that his sister was right. "Now what?"

"First, take a deep breath," she said, smiling. "Then remember what we talked about."

"Yeah," he said, his blood rushing faster, making his heart pump harder.

"Don't confront her," Gabby instructed, leaning closer. "Just act natural. Pretend nothing is wrong. *And be nice.*"

"I'm always nice."

She grinned at him. "Sure you are, big brother. In your dreams."

He hardly noticed when she took Cat from him. He was

focused on Becca, watching her welcome each and every person in the room. His only thought was that he'd done the right thing by asking her to be the party hostess. He wasn't surprised that the crew liked her. How could they not feel special each time they stopped in at the office? She was always sincerely generous with her smile and her time. He suspected she knew more about them than she did about him.

And just when would she get to him to say hello?

He felt a tug on his jacket and looked down. "Danny! I didn't see you come in."

"We all came," the boy told him. "Mom said we had to."

"Well, you wouldn't want to miss Santa, would you?"

Danny shrugged his shoulders.

Dropping down on one knee, Nick looked at the child who had won his heart and couldn't ignore the boy's grave expression. "Something bothering you, Danny?"

He shook his head, and then nodded. "Mom says we have to say goodbye tonight."

Danny's sadness made Nick want to hug him, but he held back. Becca might not appreciate it, considering. "I heard," he said, his own sadness welling inside of him.

"Will you come see us? After we move?"

Nick glanced up to see Becca working her way across the room toward them. He doubted she would agree to their friendship continuing. "If your mom says it's okay."

"She said I'll make *new* friends, but can't I still have my old friends? Like you?"

Becca interrupted before Nick could answer. "Danny, honey, somebody wants to see you."

Nick ignored her and noticed that her son did, too. "We'll work it out, Danny. Promise."

"Danny?" Becca said again, coming closer.

"Go on, now," Nick told the boy. "Go with your mom. We can talk later."

Nodding, Danny walked away to join his mom, while Nick stood, his anger rising. Gabby had told him not to confront Becca, but, dammit, he would if he didn't see a smile on Danny's face soon. He had always thought Becca was the sweetest and gentlest person he knew, but not letting Danny see him was downright mean. He wasn't going to let her get away with it.

"Trouble, boss?"

What was this, Let's Check on Nick Day? "No trouble," he grumbled. "Everything is fine."

Clint studied him. "I hear Becca's leaving."

Nick closed his eyes and counted to five. No, it was apparent that it was Let's *Dump* on Nick Day. Opening his eyes to answer, he glared at his foreman. "That's what she says."

"You gonna let her do that?"

"You think I can stop her?"

His voice had risen; several people turned to stare, and Nick wished he could disappear for a few years. Instead of escaping, he flashed them the most brilliant smile he could muster.

"The men'll mutiny, Cap'n."

Nick had to laugh, and doing so relaxed him a little. "Aye, they just might, Smee." He clapped Clint on the back. "Thanks, I needed that."

"Thought you did. Never saw you lookin' so snarly."

Snarly? He was *snarly?*

Before he could figure out exactly what that meant, his

mother waved him over. Most of his family had gathered at the table where she and his father were sitting.

"I see you're all ready to gang up on me."

His mother reached out to take his hand. "We'd never do that, Nicky."

"Oh, yeah?" He glanced around the table, faking amazement.

"We only want to see you smile. Look around," his mother said, making a sweeping gesture at the room. "All of these people are your dedicated employees. Doesn't that make you feel proud?"

He softened. "Of course it does, Mama."

"Then enjoy your accomplishments."

It was easier said than done, but Nick did try. He mingled, speaking with his employees again, charming their wives and making their children laugh. He met Martin Greshky's wife, who thanked him several times for giving her husband a job. But he didn't take his eyes off Becca and was rewarded with the proof that she was purposely avoiding him. Every time he got within six feet of her, she managed to move farther away.

Santa arrived, and Nick was pleased with his selection. He had persuaded one of his suppliers to wear the Santa suit and pass out the gifts. The role required asking for each child's name and giving him or her the correct package. With a little help from Ann-Marie, everything went smoothly, and the children were delighted, as always. If there was one thing Nick could always count on, it was his family, and he understood how envious Becca was of him.

Not long after Santa waved goodbye, jingling the bells

attached to his furry suit, people started saying their farewells and drifting out the door. Nick was sure everyone there had thanked him at least twice, and he was ready to get the event over and done with. He had always enjoyed the Christmas party, but this year, he had other things on his mind.

Within thirty minutes, everyone was gone, except the Morellis and a few employees who stayed to help clean up. It surprised Nick that Becca was among those who chose to stay, but for now, he decided to honor what he suspected were her wishes that he keep his distance. He wouldn't try to talk to her. Not yet. But he hoped the chance would present itself.

He had instructed his family to let him know when Becca walked out the door, so when he heard Gino call his name and saw him nod in that direction, Nick was ready to give it one last try. Hurrying to catch up with her, he spied her outside on her way to her car.

"Becca, wait up."

She turned, and he saw her stiffen, but she didn't walk away. "I'm sorry I wasn't here to help set up," she said when he caught up with her. "I wasn't—" She ducked her head and cleared her throat. "I was busy."

It was the weakest excuse he'd ever heard, but he wasn't going to go ballistic over it. There were more important things he needed to say.

"Where are the kids?"

"Raylene picked them up earlier, after Santa left, so I could stay to help."

Impatience radiated from her, so he cut to the chase. "The job is still yours. If you find another—"

His cell phone rang, interrupting him, and he sighed as

he dragged it out of his pocket to check the number. "I have to get this," he told her. "It's important. Please wait?"

She hesitated before giving a curt nod, and he flipped open his phone. "Any news?"

"I've found a developer for your project."

"Good, good," Nick answered, glancing at Becca.

"I think you'll be pleased. He wants to meet with you, first thing on Monday. Nine sharp."

"Tell him I'll be there." Flipping the phone closed, he turned to her. "Now, where were we?"

"If I found another job?"

"Right. If you find another job that pays better, I won't try to keep you from taking it. But I'd like for you to stay until that happens."

"I don't want to stay, Nick. I thought you were clear on that."

"No. I'm not clear on anything, and I don't think you are, either," he insisted.

"Are you telling me that I can't quit?"

He didn't like her putting words in his mouth, but that *was* what he was saying. "If that's the way you see it." When she didn't say anything, he started to worry. "Look, I know this all might seem like I was plotting against you, but—"

"Were you? Plotting against me, that is, because it does seem that way. Maybe you can explain why you deceived me for so long."

Knowing she wouldn't buy any explanation he gave her at this point, he decided it would be worthless to even try.

She stared at him for a moment. Turning, she walked away.

"Becca, I'm sorry," he said, following her. "For everything.

All I want is a few minutes to talk to you. If you'd just let me apologize for not being completely truthful and explain…"

She was at her car before he could reach her. After opening her door, she turned to look at him. "I need to pick up my children. Goodbye, Nick."

He watched, stunned, as she climbed into her car, started the engine and drove away.

Chapter Twelve

Buried in the piles of clothing she was sorting, Becca groaned at the sound of the doorbell. "Raylene, could you get the door?"

She hoped it wasn't Nick, coming to persuade her to not to quit. She'd had enough of that last night after the company Christmas party, so when she heard what she was sure was a man's voice, her heart sank. She couldn't face Nick again. Her defenses were at an all-time low. Falling back on her only option, she was leaving Katyville to find an apartment in Wichita and had hoped she wouldn't have to see Nick again. But the few apartments she had called about wanted more rent than she was willing to pay until she found a new job. Suddenly, nothing was going right in her life.

"Becca, you have guests."

Looking up, Becca nearly didn't recognize the man standing next to her best friend. "Daddy?"

She jumped to her feet and hurried over to him, not sure if she should hug him, shake his hand, or just how to greet him. When he put his arms around her, she was surprised, but didn't hesitate to return the hug.

"It's so good to see you, Daddy." Slipping out of the embrace and taking a step back, she took a long look at him. "I almost didn't recognize you. You're so tanned!"

His blue eyes twinkled when he smiled. "Those Australian beaches are wonderful. But I want you to meet someone." He turned to the woman beside him and drew her closer. "Cecily, this is my daughter, Becca."

So surprised to see her father, Becca had barely noticed the woman standing next to him. Now she was even more surprised. Cecily looked nothing like she had imagined. In her mind, she had pictured a young, curvaceous blonde, who hung on her father's every word. But the woman in front of her was far from that image. Becca guessed her to be somewhere in her forties, and not particularly curvy, but definitely not the opposite, either. Her dark hair was beautifully styled, and her smile was timid.

Remembering her manners, well taught by her mother and sometimes high-handedly encouraged by her father, Becca offered Cecily her hand. "It's wonderful to finally get to meet you."

Cecily took it, and her smile instantly warmed. "I feel the same way. Your father talks about you constantly."

"I'm just so surprised to see you both, I don't know what to say," Becca said, looking from one to the other as she released Cecily's hand.

Raylene, who had moved to stand next to her, leaned close. "You might ask them to sit down," she whispered.

"Oh! Yes, of course." Becca wondered what kind of impression she was giving them as she led them into her living room. Grabbing a pile of clothes from the sofa, she dumped them on the floor. "You'll have to excuse the mess. I'm packing."

Raylene dumped another pile from a chair, but Becca continued to stand. Shrugging, Raylene sat on it instead.

"Packing for what?" her father asked as he settled on the sofa next to his wife.

"A move."

"You're moving?"

"Yes, into Wichita, I hope. I've been working in Katyville, but I've decided to take another job in the city. Living near it will make commuting easier." She hoped she had made it sound as if it were her choice and that she was excited.

Cecily leaned forward. "What kind of work have you been doing?"

Becca quickly glanced at Raylene for moral support. "I've been the secretary for a local construction company."

"You didn't tell me you had a job," her father said.

Nerves had her clearing her throat. The last thing she wanted to do was explain everything that had been happening. In fact, she couldn't. To do so might cause more problems with her father, and she wasn't willing to risk that. "I wasn't working when we spoke on the phone," she admitted.

His eyebrows shot up. "That was barely three weeks ago."

Forcing a smile, she nodded. "Yes, isn't it amazing? I was offered the job the next day, and I've been working there ever since."

"And you're already taking a new one?"

She grasped for the first thing that came to mind. "I have a glowing recommendation from the owner, and I thought—" She quickly searched her mind for a plausible explanation. "I thought it might be nice for the kids to live in the city, instead of stuck out here in a small town."

"Stuck?" her father echoed.

"Well, not 'stuck,' but there are advantages to schools in the city. More technology and all that. And Danny will be starting kindergarten in the fall, so..."

Her father's eyes narrowed as he studied her. "It's a bit sudden, isn't it? Is money that much of a problem?"

Her knees weakened under her father's scrutiny, and she felt the need to sit. Perching on a stack of pillows on the fireplace hearth, she gathered her strength and shook her head. "It isn't that. The house has sold to a new owner, and we've been asked to leave."

"Mrs. Watkins sold this place?" Her father looked around the room. "I never thought she'd do that. Who did she sell it to?"

Panic silenced Becca, but Raylene took over. "A corporation out of Denver."

His eyes opened wide. "Whatever for?"

Cecily touched his arm. "Now, Jock, if Becca wants to move, that's her decision."

He opened his mouth to speak, but quickly closed it. "You're right." Turning to Becca, he said, "If you need any help finding a place to live or money for deposit or down payment, I'll be happy to help." Beside him, Cecily nodded, smiling, and gave his arm a loving squeeze.

Becca couldn't believe what she was hearing. Her father had never been willing to help with anything. Except to pick her husband, and that had been a disaster. "Thank you, Daddy. And Cecily, too."

Raylene pushed to her feet. "Can I get you some coffee, Mr. and Mrs. Malone?"

"It's Cecily, please," Becca's stepmother answered. "And I'd love some, but I have to pass. We can't stay long."

"And I'm Jock," Becca's father said to Raylene. "We're all grown-ups now. No reason for this Mr. and Mrs. nonsense."

"You can't leave yet," Becca told them. "You just arrived."

"Only for a little while," her father said. "I want to head up to Kansas City to visit your Aunt Judith later today. We'll stay overnight and be back in the morning."

"How long will you two be here then?"

"Until after the New Year," Cecily answered. "I have family in Florida that I want to stop and visit before we return home, but we wanted to see you first, if only for a few minutes."

Becca relaxed. "You're welcome to stay here. We have lots of room, but I might put you to work with the packing."

"If you need the help, we're here to do that," her father replied.

Becca wasn't sure the man sitting on her sofa was really her father. He had changed. Was Cecily the reason for that? Wanting to get to know her stepmother a little better, Becca was slightly disappointed that they would be leaving, if only for a short time. "But you'll be back for Christmas Eve, right? I know the kids will be excited."

"Speaking of your children," Cecily began, "are they here? I've wanted to meet them for so long."

"April and Daisy are napping upstairs, but they should wake up soon," Becca explained. "Danny is doing some last-minute shopping with Raylene's husband and will be home later."

Her father stood. "If I'm quiet, would you mind if I look in on them?"

"Of course not," Becca answered. "And if April and Daisy wake up, it won't hurt."

Raylene jumped to her feet. "Let me show you the way, uh, Jock, while Becca and Cecily get to know each other."

They left the room, heading up the stairs, and once they were gone, Cecily scooted to the end of the sofa, closer to Becca. "I'll wait until we get back to spend time with the children, when they're up and awake. I'm looking forward to spending time with them," she said. "And you. I've been wanting to talk to you for so long, but—" She smiled and placed her hand on Becca's. "I know your father has been somewhat…well, overbearing in the past," she said, glancing toward the staircase, "but he's very proud of you. And I think you'll find that he's able to show that now. He does love you."

Becca's throat closed with the tears that threatened. "Thank you," she murmured and squeezed Cecily's hand. "That means a lot to me."

Cecily's smile was understanding. "It was very hard on your father to lose your mother, as I'm sure it was for you, too. It took me a long time to break through that brick wall he'd put around his heart. To tell the truth, he still has a ways to go, but he's trying."

"You're obviously very good for him."

"I try to be. He does need someone to remind him now and then not to bite off everyone's head."

Becca spied Raylene and her father returning. "Were

you born in Australia?" she asked Cecily, knowing neither of them wanted her father to know about their conversation.

Cecily smiled at her husband, before turning back to Becca. "No, here in the States. New Mexico, actually. I married young and was widowed not long after. I needed to get away and decided a trip to Australia would be the thing to get me through it all. As soon as I arrived in Sydney, I knew I couldn't leave."

"And speaking of leaving," Becca's father said, "I hate to say it, but if we're driving to Kansas City, we need to get started."

Cecily agreed, and they gathered their things. At the door, Becca hugged her. "I wish you didn't have to go so soon. You'll be back tomorrow, right?"

"You can count on it," her father said, "but I can't make any promises about what time."

Becca smiled at him. "We'll see you when you get here."

He stepped closer. Placing his palm on her cheek, he sighed. "I probably haven't told you this, but you've grown into a beautiful woman. And I don't worry about smarts. You've always had plenty of those." And then he wrapped her in his arms, kissing her cheek. "Thanks for liking Ceci," he whispered.

"She's wonderful," Becca whispered back. "I'm so glad you found her."

As Becca and Raylene waved goodbye, Becca truly hated to see them go. "He's changed," she said, as the car disappeared down the road.

"He found a good woman," Raylene agreed. "Another one, I should say. Sometimes that's what it takes." She turned to Becca and draped her arm across her shoulders. "Now we just need to fix things for you."

Becca did her best to smile. "I'm fine. Really." But she knew it was a lie. She wished she knew how to make everything better and suspected time would do the trick. Time and distance.

NICK SAT IN FRONT of the television at his parents' house. It was turned on, but the sound was off. He wasn't really watching, but at least he appeared to be doing something. His family was due to arrive home at any minute from Christmas Eve services at the church, and he had to at least make it look like he wasn't brooding. He was sick of the looks they all kept giving him. If there was one thing he hated more than anything, it was pity.

Besides, what was so pitiful about him? His unwillingness to tell Becca that he was her landlord had pretty much set him free. She was stubborn, he told himself, and a stubborn woman could make a man's life miserable. She was unyielding and wouldn't even let him explain—not that he had a good reason for not telling her right off the bat. But she was distrustful, at least when it came to him. She would never trust him again. But he couldn't blame her for that.

He closed his eyes and tipped his head back. He knew he wasn't being fair, but anger had gotten him through their first breakup. Maybe it would again. Something had to.

He had screwed up. Royally. He'd done everything he knew to do, and he'd failed. Now he had to live with it. That's the way consequences worked.

"Nicky, we're home."

As if he couldn't tell, what with all the noise in the foyer.

Opening his eyes, he watched the parade of people pass through the living room. Everybody from his parents to the smallest of his nieces and nephews passed by him, each trying not to look at him. He was even sure he could hear his name being bandied about in the kitchen.

"Would you like some eggnog, Nicky?"

He shook his head and continued to stare at the soundless screen in front of him.

"Nico, answer your mother with some respect."

Nick glanced up to see his father standing to his left. "No, thank you, Mama," he said, but didn't bother to look at her.

He must have been crazy to think he could come back to Katyville and have a life that his entire family wasn't involved in. Nothing ever changed. In the Morelli family, nobody hesitated to stick their nose in everybody else's business. Becca might think having a big family was a plus all the time, but she didn't know the truth.

He winced. Truth was something he wanted to think less about. As if he'd let it bother him before.

He didn't know how long he sat there, while everyone else went about setting up for the holiday celebration, but he suddenly realized that the house was quiet. Out of the corner of his eye, he saw his mother standing in the dining room, huddled with Gabby.

Here we go. They must have decided it was time to cheer up poor Nick. He swiped his hand down his face and breathed out a sigh.

One by one they joined him in the living room. He did his best to ignore them and remained silent, even though he knew what was coming.

"Are you watching this?" Angelo asked him, his finger on the off button of the TV. He pushed the button before Nick had a chance to answer. "I didn't think so."

Nick glared at him, but his brother didn't seem to notice.

Pushing out of the chair, Nick got to his feet. "I think I'll go up to my room. You all have a good time."

He hadn't taken two steps when his mother stopped him. "Sit down, Nicky. If you forgot, it's Christmas Eve, and this family spends it together."

As if he could forget. He'd had big plans for this night. Major, life-changing plans.

Instead of making excuses, he returned to the chair and lowered himself onto it. "Let the games begin," he announced.

His father shot him a warning look, but his mother only shook her head. "Is that what this is, Nicky? A game?"

"I don't know, Mama. If it is, I'm losing."

He tried not to notice the looks they all exchanged, and then they were all on him at once, each in his or her own way assuring him that he wasn't. Gabby sat on the arm of his chair and somehow managed to slip her arm around him. "It's the fourth quarter and you're down six with fifteen seconds to play," she told him.

He almost smiled. He'd loved playing football, but had never been good enough to win a scholarship for it.

Joseph smiled and went to stand beside his wife. "The huddle's over. It's fourth down and the wide receiver is out with an injury. *You've* been chosen to catch the pass from the quarterback."

Nick nodded. He'd been a running back and hadn't done a half-bad job of it.

Tony continued the commentary. "The cheerleaders are chanting your name."

Nick chuckled.

"The teams jostle for position on the scrimmage line, ready for the signal," Gino said, joining the others. "Twenty yards, that's all you need."

"The crowd in the stadium is so loud, you can barely hear the quarterback—"

"But you do," Beth finishes for Ann-Marie. "And the next thing you know, you're down the field and the ball is in the air, headed straight for you."

Karen perched on the other side of him. "So what do you do? Do you put your hands up to catch it?"

"Or do you stand there and let it fly over the top of you, passing you by? Which is it, Nick?" Angelo asked him.

Nick didn't even have to think. "I see your point." Nodding, he got to his feet. "Time to catch the ball."

He left the house with his own cheering squad shouting encouragement to him in the dark. It was nearly ten o'clock, but he hoped Becca would give him a break. If his family hadn't made him see that he would only lose—everyone would lose—if he didn't stay in the game, he wouldn't be driving to her house. Maybe being a part of a big family was as great as he had always thought. If Becca refused to talk to him, he knew his family wouldn't let him give up and would stand by him, no matter what happened.

He almost lost his nerve when he pulled into her drive and saw a car with rental plates on it. Then he decided it didn't matter who was there. He would have his say.

Becca opened the door when he rang the bell. "Go home and be with your family, Nick," she told him.

Nick stood his ground. "Talk to me now or I won't stop until you do."

"Who is it, Becca?"

Nick heard the man's voice, and his heart sank. He almost turned to leave, but when he saw Jock Malone step up behind Becca, it stopped him cold. The other team had put in a ringer.

"It's Nick Morelli, Mr. Malone," Nick answered for her.

"Well, let him in, Becca," Jock said. "It's cold out there. I'm sure he didn't drive out here to be left standing on the porch."

"I only need a few minutes to talk to Becca," Nick explained.

"Take all the time you want," Jock told him over his shoulder as he walked away, leaving them alone.

Nick was speechless. The man who had put a stop to their relationship ten years earlier seemed to now be giving him what he needed. "Becca?" Nick asked, when she didn't move.

Her eyes closed for a moment, and when she opened them, she swung the door open. "You have one minute."

He started to protest as he stepped inside the house, but decided it would only waste precious seconds. "First, I didn't tell you right off that I owned the house, because I was in a state of shock at seeing you again. Second, I sensed you needed a little help, and you wouldn't have let me do that if you had known."

She was silent, so he took a deep breath. "Third, I offered you the job because I needed someone immediately and I knew it would help you out. I think it has, and it helped me, too. Fourth, as soon as I discovered you were the renter, I gave instructions that your checks were not to be cashed. And fifth," he continued, "it all comes down to wanting to help because I love you. Now, where are the kids? We're going to spend Christmas Eve with my family."

Becca lowered her head. "You love my children, not me."

He couldn't believe she was saying that. "Wrong again, sweetheart. You are the bravest, strongest woman I know. Not to mention the most stubborn."

Shaking her head, she turned away. "First my father controlled me, then my husband." She swung around to face him. "Even you, although I don't believe you meant to. Just how brave and strong is that?"

"You've been pulling my strings for more than three weeks now. Everything I've done since I found you with that flat tire has been for you. So just who's doing the controlling?" he asked with a grin.

"I only want to control my own life. Is that too much to ask?"

"No. And I only wanted to give you the tools to do it." When she didn't reply, he walked to the stairs and looked up, then turned back to her. "Are they asleep yet?"

"I doubt it. After all, it *is* Christmas Eve."

"Then come on," he said, starting up the stairs. "Let's get them dressed."

"They're not going anywhere. They're in bed, Nick, dreaming of sugarplums or whatever. Or soon will be, I hope."

He turned around and headed back down the stairs, stopping in front of her and taking her shoulders in his hands. This might be his only chance, and he knew he had to give it his all. "Becca—" He stopped and closed his eyes, then opened them before speaking again. "Don't you understand? I want them there. I want *you* there. I want to spend Christmas Eve with you. All of you. Otherwise, there's nothing to celebrate. Not for me, anyway."

She twisted out of his grasp and turned away from him. "Not tonight, Nick. Don't you see?" she said, turning back. "I don't want their hearts broken. They've become so attached to you that when the time comes that you aren't here for them anymore, they'll be crushed. I can't let that happen."

He raked his hair with his hand in frustration. She didn't understand that this wasn't some temporary thing. He wanted it to be forever, but this wasn't the time or the place to tell her. He had to show her that she could be a part of his family, just as he wanted to become part of hers. If only he could get her to join them all tonight, she would see—

"Give the man a chance, Becca," Jock said from behind them. "Heaven knows I didn't."

"Mom, did you see this?"

Becca looked again at the tool set Nick had given her son. It was sized for a small boy, and Danny hadn't been able to put it down since he had unwrapped it.

"Yes, honey, it's wonderful," she told him. "But you'll have to be careful and learn how to use everything correctly."

Danny's head bobbed in a nod. "I know. Nick'll teach me." He looked at Nick. "Won't you?"

"You bet," Nick answered, reaching out to lay a hand on his shoulder.

When Danny ran off to join the rest of the Morelli off-spring, she turned to Nick. "You do realize how lucky you are, don't you?"

"Completely."

She sighed, knowing he had no idea what she was

talking about. "I mean this." She pointed to the Morelli living room, filled with laughing people and discarded wrapping paper and boxes.

"Oh, that," Nick answered, grinning. The grin disappeared and was replaced by a more serious expression. "Yeah, I do know how lucky I am. In a lot of ways."

She was grateful to Nick for insisting she come with him, but she was even more grateful to her father for admitting his past mistake of driving Nick out of her life. If things had been different… But they hadn't been, and it was time to move on.

The drive to Nick's parents' house had been short and left little time to talk, what with three children who had been taken from their beds and dressed in a rush in the backseat of her car. Now that she'd had some time to think, there were questions that needed answers. With everyone busy and the spotlight finally off of her and Nick, it seemed to be the right time to ask.

"Why my house, Nick? Or maybe I should say your house."

He was silent for a moment, staring straight ahead. "I told you the story about how Corey and I sneaked in to check it out."

"But why buy it?"

He shrugged, and she sensed his hesitation, but she hoped he would eventually tell her.

"Ever since that night with Corey and even before, I've had a fascination with it. There was something special about it, but I've never been able to put my finger on it."

"It's a good house."

He turned to look at her, smiling. "It's a great house. And maybe that's it. Maybe."

"Do you go around buying all the great houses you see?"

"This is the first one. I can't promise it won't be the last though." He turned to face her. "You see, it has character, like this one. This house has made it through almost thirty-five years of marriage and six kids, and it's still as good as the day Pop bought it."

"You told me, one night a long time ago, that someday the Watkins place would be yours, and you would make it a showplace."

"I remember," he said, his voice nearly a whisper. "It was raining, and we were parked down the road from it."

Emotions knotted in her throat at the memory. "That wasn't the only time. There were more."

"I know there were. I remember them all. And I will make it a showplace, Becca," he said. "Everybody has a dream, and that house has always been mine. But it's only a part of it."

She wasn't sure he would share, but she had to ask. She needed to know. "What are the others?"

He leaned back and closed his eyes, a soft smile touching his lips. "A family like my parents gave us. A house filled with love and laughter. And a little battle, now and then," he added, opening one eye to look at her, and then the other. "I want children. They're the lifeblood of a family. My parents are proof of that."

Haunted by his draw to her children, she looked down to stare at her hands. "Is that why you're so drawn to Danny and April and—"

"No. Not because I wanted them to be my family, although I wouldn't mind that. It's because they're great kids. And I'm crazy about kids. Maybe because my own childhood was so good."

Becca looked around for her children. Daisy was safely sleeping upstairs in a nursery with Gabby and Joseph's tiny son, and she finally spied Danny and April, laughing and playing with the others, their eyes shining with delight and a joy she hadn't seen in a long time. This was the kind of family she had always wished hers had been.

Cat's sudden shout filled the house. "Mommy, Mommy! Snow!"

Beside her, Nick groaned. "As if we didn't have enough two weeks ago."

"But it's Christmas, Nick," Becca reminded him, feeling more in the spirit of the holiday. "We'll have a white Christmas. What could be better than that?"

His gaze met hers for a moment, unreadable. "You're right, of course." He stood and held out his hand. She took it and let him lead her outside with the rest of his family.

"It's coming down pretty good," Angelo said, while his son stood on the steps and stuck out his tongue to catch snowflakes.

"It's so pretty," Beth agreed, pressing her pregnant middle against the porch railing and leaning out to catch flakes in her hand.

Nick put his arm around Becca's waist, pulling her close. She didn't resist, needing to be near him, if only for a while. In spite of everything Nick had said, she wasn't convinced he wanted the forever that she dreamed of, so she was making memories to take with her.

"It's getting cold," someone behind them grumbled.

"Time to get the little ones inside," Elena said. "Nobody needs a chill for Christmas."

Realizing everyone was going back into the house,

Becca turned to follow the others inside. Nick caught her hand and gently pulled her back, wrapping his arms around her from behind as they gazed at the beauty in front of them.

Becca had never felt so happy yet so sad at the same time. No matter where she went or what happened, this night would remain in her memory forever. "I envy you so, Nick Morelli," she whispered. "To grow up in a family so filled with love had to be special. It must be why you are, too."

"Why did you move to the Watkins place?" he asked her, his breath warming against her hair.

The question came from nowhere and surprised her. "Because I could afford it," she told him. "And because it held memories, too, I think. Why did you buy it?"

He turned her until she was facing him, his arms still encircling her. "You are the most important reason I bought the house."

"Me?"

"Yes, you." He kissed the tip of her nose.

Afraid to believe what he was saying, she shook her head.

"Do you remember how we dreamed about sharing our lives in it, once I finished college? We had our lives planned out. Together."

"I remember," she whispered. "I never forgot." And it seemed that Nick hadn't, either, even though she had thought he had.

He gazed down at her, as a golden glow from inside lit their corner of the porch. "Everyone has been hinting that the family needs to be bigger," he said.

Becca laughed, but didn't look away. "I think Beth and Tony are doing a good job of that."

"Yeah, they are, but…" He shifted his weight and pulled her even closer. "Becca," he whispered, "I always wanted that house for us. That was our dream."

"But—"

He pressed a finger to her lips. "You know how much I love your kids. They're very special to me. But what you don't understand is that what makes them so special is that they're a part of you."

She ducked her head, not knowing what to say. Her heart drummed in her chest and breathing was difficult.

Tipping up her face with a finger under her chin, Nick smiled. "Becca, I love you. I've loved you all these years. That's why I went away when we broke up. I couldn't stay if I couldn't have you."

"Nick—"

"Let me finish. When I saw you that night on the road, I was angry. But it wasn't with you. It was with myself for still loving you. There you were, the wife of another man, or at least that's what I thought, and all those old feelings were surfacing, and I didn't know how to deal with them."

Fighting back tears, she managed to speak. "Nick, you don't have to tell me."

"Yeah, I do, because I'm just now figuring this out."

"But I understand. I've done the same things."

He stared at her. "You have?"

Smiling, she nodded. "I love you, too, Nick."

"Then why—"

"I told you. I was afraid Danny and April would be hurt. Daisy, too."

He let out a long breath. "I'd never do that."

She could see the honesty in his eyes, and her heart

opened. This was the man she had always needed. Her heart had known it all along. Lifting her hand, she pressed it to his face. "I know."

He placed his hand over hers. "But you have to be careful. I understand that."

She nodded and laid her head on his chest. His heart beat strongly, and she knew she had nothing to fear from him. For the first time in years, she felt safe. Loved.

"There's just one more thing," he said.

Moving away just enough to look up at him, she asked, "What's that?"

Movement caused her to look down, and she saw his closed hand between them. Slowly, he opened it. She gasped at the sight of a brilliant diamond ring, sparkling in the light from the house.

"Will you marry me, Becca Malone Tyler?"

His voice was rough with emotion, and her eyes filled with tears. Unable to speak, she nodded. "Anytime, anywhere," she finally managed to say.

Taking her hand, he slipped the ring on her finger, and they both were silent. When she looked up at him, she was crying, but they were tears of joy.

He gathered her in his arms again, kissing her deeply, and she responded with all the love she had carried in her heart for so many years. When they both came up for air, he glanced over his shoulder.

"What's wrong?" she asked, standing on her toes to see what he was looking at.

"Nobody interrupted us."

Laughing, she surrendered herself for another toe-curling kiss, wishing they'd never have to stop. When they finally did, he held her close, and she listened to the even rhythm of his heart, calming her and assuring her that her life and her children's would be filled with love and laughter.

"Oh, one more thing," he said.

She leaned back to look at him. "What's that?"

"Big Sky Construction will start work on a low-income apartment complex later this year. It's my Christmas present to you."

Becca swallowed the tears that kept her from speaking and pressed her face to his chest, breathing in the scent of the man she loved. The man she had always loved.

"It's stopped snowing," he said, and Becca turned in his arms to see.

A light blanket of snow covered the ground, twinkling in the glow of distant streetlights. Above, the clouds were beginning to clear.

"Look at that," he said, pointing to the sky.

Safe and secure in Nick's arms, Becca watched a falling star until it disappeared. "Thank you," she whispered.

Silhouette® Desire

NEW YORK TIMES BESTSELLING AUTHOR

DIANA PALMER

A brand-new Long, Tall Texans novel

IRON COWBOY

*Available March 2008
wherever you buy books.*

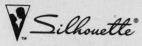

Romantic
SUSPENSE

Sparked by Danger, Fueled by Passion.

When Tech Sergeant Jacob "Mako" Stone opens his door to a mysterious woman without a past, he knows his time off is over. As threats to Dee's life bring her and Jacob together, she must set aside her pride and accept the help of the military hero with too many secrets of his own.

Out of Uniform
by Catherine Mann

Available February wherever you buy books.

$1.00 OFF

The bestselling Lakeshore Chronicles continue with *Snowfall at Willow Lake*, a story of what comes after a woman survives an unspeakable horror and finds her way home, to healing and redemption and a new chance at happiness.

SUSAN WIGGS

On sale February 2008!

SAVE $1.00

off the purchase price of **SNOWFALL AT WILLOW LAKE** by Susan Wiggs.

Offer valid from February 1, 2008, to April 30, 2008.
Redeemable at participating retail outlets. Limit one coupon per purchase.

® and TM are trademarks owned and used by the trademark owner and/or its licensee.
© 2008 Harlequin Enterprises Limited

MSW2493CPN

Texas Hold 'Em

When it comes to love, the stakes are high

Sixteen years ago, Luke Chisum dated
Becky Parker on a dare…before going
on to break her heart. Now the former
River Bluff daredevil is back, rekindling
desire and tempting Becky to pick up
where they left off. But this time she has
to resist or Luke could discover the secret
she's kept locked away all these years.…

Look for

Texas Bluff

by Linda Warren

#1470

*Available February 2008
wherever you buy books.*

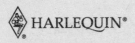

HARLEQUIN®

American ★ Romance®

COMING NEXT MONTH

#1197 THE FAMILY PLAN by Cathy McDavid
Fatherhood
It's an emotional homecoming for injured show rider Jolyn Sutherland...
especially when she runs into veterinarian Chase Raintree, her secret
girlhood crush. This time around, he seems to return the feeling. But a crisis
involving Jolyn's family and Chase's eight-year-old daughter could derail their
relationship before it gets off the ground....

#1198 UNEXPECTED BRIDE by Lisa Childs
The Wedding Party
Only her best friend's wedding could bring Abby Hamilton back to her Michigan
hometown. But when the bride runs away, sparks fly between Abby and Clayton
McClintock, a man she always admired...even when he thought she was nothing
but trouble. Could it be that the people of Cloverdale will get to see a wedding
after all?

#1199 THE RIGHT MR. WRONG by Cindi Myers
Everyone in Crested Butte, Colorado, has warned Maddie Alexander about the
good-looking Hagan Ansdar. His no-commitment views make him an *in*eligible
bachelor. Good thing she's immune to Mr. Wrong...or is she? Because when
Hagan pursues her, she finds it hard to resist!

#1200 IN A SOLDIER'S ARMS by Marin Thomas
Hearts of Appalachia
When Maggie O'Neil goes home to the family birthplace, Heather's Hollow,
she's expecting to find out all the clan's secrets from a grandmother who claims
every O'Neil woman has "second sight." Maggie doesn't believe a word of
it—until she meets ex-soldier Abram Devane and "sees" her future—with him!

www.eHarlequin.com

HARCNM0108